# PRAISE FOR "BETRAYAL IN OKLAHOMA"

"This story is gripping, the pace is deliciously fast, and Sara's personality is perfect. She's spunky, funny, stubborn, and loyal, and entirely, completely likable.

"And, after reading this delightful novella from her adventures, I want more!"

-*THE INTERNATIONAL REVIEW OF BOOKS*

"Loved it! Strong female character, interesting take on werewolves, with a satisfying ending.

"This was a refreshingly original take on the werewolf mythos. Sue Denver has written a fascinating character in Sara. She reminds me of Jane Yellowrock from Faith Hunter's series, and in all the right ways: strong, aloof, in control of herself (until she isn't), mysterious, and a loner. Shifting is dealt with as a practical reality rather than magic and sparkles, and I'm down with that."

"Although the theme of the story is dark, Sara's interactions with her canine companion Skidi add lighter moments that show glimpses of their history and the strength of their bond.

"*Betrayal in Oklahoma* should appeal to anyone who likes seeing bad guys brought to justice, loves shifters, likes strong female characters who aren't obsessed by hunky men, and prefers werewolves that don't fit the standard paranormal romance tropes."

-MJ SILVERSMITH, *REEDSY DISCOVERY*

## PRAISE FOR AMATEUR ASSASSIN

"This is a fast-read novella with strong prose, and a plot that moves briskly along. The main character, Sara Flores is, well, a werewolf. I liked the fact that this important piece of information about Sara was stated right at the beginning of the story. There's no puzzling about whether this is actually a possible condition, or whether it's a believable situation. Instead, it's just who Sara is and what she does.

"And because Sara is a werewolf, her senses are more finely tuned than the average human, which is an integral aspect of the story. Her enhanced olfactory abilities compel her to follow a woman (who she dubs Mystery Woman), which in turn leads Sara to a grisly murder scene. Mystery Woman, who is gravely wounded, entrusts the future of the world to Sara. She has foisted an almost impossible ethical dilemma on Sara — should someone die in the present for their future transgressions? That type of earth-changing dilemma.

"If you're the type of reader who, like me, is willing to accept the unusual and quirky in a book, this will be an enjoyable read for you. If you like a story that moves along at a good clip, you'll enjoy this book. And if you like strong, decisive characters, then you will enjoy *Amateur Assassin*. Read it! It's fun!"

TESS QUINN, *REEDSY DISCOVERY*

## PRAISE FOR THE STENCH OF FEAR

"While I originally thought, 'A werewolf? Really??' I got into the story and thoroughly enjoyed it. This novella is a wild ride of confrontations as well as dangerous situations and dishonest cops. I was riveted. The writing was excellent and I felt as if I were totally in Sara's shoes, feeling her anger, guilt and power as she tries to discover who she can trust and who she can't. Highly recommended!"

*-THE INTERNATIONAL REVIEW OF BOOKS*

"Two can keep a secret — if one of them is dead. Are there dirty cops on the force? What happens when you trust the wrong person? I give *The Stench of Fear: A Paranormal Mystery Novella* by Sue Denver 5 out of 5 stars for the author's larger than life main character and for providing an incredible point-of-view werewolf style. Warning this novella contains some graphic explicit content.

-WYMANETTE CASTANEDA, *REEDSY DISCOVERY*

# WEREWOLF VIGILANTE

BOOK 2 OF SARA FLORES, THE EARLY YEARS

SUE DENVER

 JGF PRESS

*Werewolf Vigilante*

**Includes 3 novellas:**

- ***Betrayal in Oklahoma***
- ***The Stench of Fear***
- ***Amateur Assassin***

All published by JGF Press, at JGFpress.com

Websites: SueDenver.com and WolfLady.net

It should go without saying, given this is a book about a werewolf, but just in case(!)... This book is a work of fiction. Names, characters, places, and incidents are a product of the author's imagination. Real locales and public and celebrity names are sometimes used for atmospheric purposes. Any resemblance to actual people, living or dead, or to businesses, companies, tribes, events, institutions, or places, is either coincidental or used in a fictional manner.

Published November 8, 2022 by JGF Press, Crossville TN

# SARA FLORES' WORLD
## WHAT YOU SHOULD KNOW

- Sara's world is our everyday, normal world.
- Nobody believes in werewolves, vampires or anything supernatural.
- Sara was turned into a werewolf by her former neighbor Joe White Wolf — right before he died.
- Sara thinks she's the only werewolf on earth — but she hopes she's wrong.
- Lupiti elders remember their grandfathers talk about seeing old Joe White Wolf turn into a wolf during tribal ceremonies back in the late 1800's.
- This tells Sara she may have a very, very long life, if her new lifestyle doesn't get her killed

# CONTENTS

# INTRODUCTION

It's been two years since Sara Flores jumped inside my head and took over so much of my life.

I always loved writing fiction and I always loved wolves — but mom and dad raised a "practical" woman and I went into business instead. For decades.

...Until the day I "met" Sara and she refused to take no for an answer. (She's pushy that way!)

"If not now — when?" she asked me. A very good question.

Could I actually spend my days imagining my life as a real wolf? Could I earn a living saving people and beating up on bad guys? From the safety of my home?

I decided to take the gamble.

My early stories of Sara got good reviews, but next-to-no sales. Seriously. We're talking one sale every 2-3 weeks!

Meanwhile Sara kept getting stronger in my head. Soon I moved from writing short stories to writing novellas about her. Now she's demanding full novels for her adventures. And a team of characters around her.

I combined her first eight adventures (seven short stories and one novella) into a collection called *Newbie Werewolf*. And I spent the huge sum (for me) of $315 on advertising it.

The advertising sold 226 books over four days, after which the sales stopped dead for a week. Then a funny thing happened. With no more advertising, I was suddenly selling a book a day. Then two books a day, then three. It's continuing to grow.

I was gobsmacked!

Granted, I'm no competitor to Dean Koontz, Nora Roberts, Patricia Briggs or Lee Child. They can rest easy.

But... it meant the world to me that others wanted to read about Sara. That they told their friends about her. And their friends told their friends.

This compilation of three novellas are Sara's Year-2 adventures. She's learning, growing, and dealing with ever bigger bad guys.

What's in the future? Sara decided to get her P.I. license in *The Stench of Fear*, included here. That caused me to start a new series with her, titled SARA FLORES, WEREWOLF P.I.

Let me conclude by thanking you for making my (and Sara's) dreams come true. Each morning I get to put my feet up on my desk, my laptop in my lap, and run away to imaginary worlds. Where men are men and women are — werewolves?

Thank you!
Sue

Author of *Newbie Werewolf* and *A Werewolf at the Zoo?*

# SUE DENVER

## Betrayal in Oklahoma

A WolfLady™ Paranormal Adventure Novella

# ONE

Betrayal in Oklahoma
By Sue Denver

Karl Nilsson looked everywhere for the missing boy. He was getting very worried. He'd rubbed his fingers through his gray hair, patted his mustache, and smoothed his goatee — all nervous habits he was trying to overcome. Which he knew would never happen today of all days.

Unfortunately, there were a lot of places for a three-year-old to hide on his sister's ranch here in Smithville, Oklahoma. The nearest neighbors were a mile away on either side, but the place was mostly surrounded by woods. Karl had already looked in Lucas' messy room, in the horse barn and in their three sheds. He was running out of likely places. Worried Lucas might be hidden somewhere in the woods, Karl moved behind the barn — and there he was. Lucas was playing. Playing in the mud with the family lapdog, Princess.

The boy's white-blond hair was streaked with mud, and his jeans were caked in it. His t-shirt looked like he'd done a belly flop in the muck.

Karl started to smile. Then he stopped. He looked around. They were out of sight of the house — a big stroke of luck. The woods started about 70 feet away, and it was probably another 100-120 feet to the river. Where the men would be waiting.

Karl had until noon, but this was his best chance.

"Lucas," Karl said. The boy stopped quickly. He looked up and tried to look innocent. On a three-year-old, the result was laughably guilty.

"Uncle Karl," the boy said. "Princess got in the mud. I help her."

Karl looked at Princess. The white mixed-breed fluff ball was even muddier than the boy — he couldn't see a spec that was still white. But... Karl's nose flinched. From the pungent odor coming off the dog, mud wasn't the only thing she'd rolled in. Karl made himself smile fully.

"That's very good of you," he said, nodding. "Guess what I found?"

"What?"

"A nest of baby rabbits."

"Where?"

"Right over there," Karl said, pointing towards the woods. "Right by that tree there."

"Can I see?"

"Sure. Let's go look."

Lucas started running towards the woods, but then he stopped.

"I'm not s'pposed to go there," he said, looking down.

"It's OK. I'll come with you." Karl came up beside the boy.

Lucas reached up and took Karl's hand. "Let's go!"

Karl swallowed. The feel of the boy's tiny, trusting hand in his... He was distracted when Princess shook herself all over, sending mud and who knew what else flying over both of them.

"Bad dog, Princess," said Lucas. But he was giggling. "Uncle Karl — you got muddy!"

"What?" asked Karl. *Was the dog going to be a problem?*

"You're muddy!" Lucas said.

Karl tamped down his impatience and took an exaggerated look at himself. "You're right. Let's hurry before your mom sees us and smacks both our bottoms!" Karl started them towards the trees, as fast as the boy's little legs would carry him. The ground was packed so their feet didn't sink in. But it was chopped up from horse hooves. He had to lift the boy's arm occasionally to prevent him from tripping.

Lucas was laughing while he ran.

"Smack *both* our bottoms!" he said. "Mama's gonna smack *your* bottom too!"

They reached the edge of the woods.

"Where are the rabbits?" Lucas asked.

"It's just a little farther."

Lucas stopped. He looked back towards the horse barn and suddenly looked worried. Karl could see trouble coming.

"They're just over there," he said, pointing into the woods. "Want to ride piggy back to see them?"

"Yes!"

Karl ordered the dog to stay. Princess whined but lay down obediently on the ground.

Karl crossed his arms and took the boy's wrists. He swung him around onto his back and fastened the kid's arms around his neck. He got a good grip on the boy's legs and moved forward again.

Karl was surprised — he was unusually clumsy moving through the woods. He kept bumping into one tree after another. He had to be more careful — or the boy would cry out. He realized his vision was blurry. He blinked his eyes and was shocked to feel tears running down his cheeks.

Karl reached the edge of the woods and looked around. A once-yellow two-seat canoe was pulled up on the bank 20 feet downriver. Two men were beside it with fishing poles out. Pretending. They looked like a couple of down-at-heel Okies with a handed-down canoe — but Karl knew better. The boat might look scruffy, but he bet it was in perfect shape under the faded paint.

Grady was there, looking like an average Joe in every way, including sandy hair starting to recede. He was dressed down as much as he could be without actually wearing cheap clothes. Grady appeared to be the kind of guy you'd never notice — unless you crossed him. Then you'd sure-by-damn notice him.

Grady's man was there too — a wiry, twitchy runt named Ryder. Karl had thought it funny at first — the "muscle" of the team being so small and lightweight compared to Grady. But one look in Ryder's eyes explained it to Karl. There wasn't anybody home in those eyes. At least, not anybody you'd ever want to meet.

Grady had explained last night, in excruciating detail, just what would happen to Karl if he didn't do this. Karl shuddered, remembering. He'd decided then and there he had no choice. Unless he was willing to eat his gun. Which he wasn't.

But now... the boy... His sister would be devastated. Karl steeled himself. She could have another kid, couldn't she? But he couldn't get another life.

Besides, the kid would have a good new home. With a family rich enough to buy anything they — or the kid — want.

"Here are the bunnies," he said to Lucas, loud enough to carry, as he ran to the canoe.

The men turned towards him. They separated and both moved towards him.

Karl slung Lucas to the ground and pointed into the boat. Grady had reached into his pocket and pulled out a syringe. He grabbed the boy and stuck it into his arm.

Lucas waved his hands and tried to get away. "No! No!" he cried out.

Grady lifted him and put the squirming, wriggling boy in the boat.

Grady looked around. "OK," he said, reaching into his jacket. He pulled out two papers and handed them to Karl. "You wanted these," he said. "You might take better care of them in the future!"

Karl grabbed the papers, his hand shaking. He put them inside his shirt to protect them, petting them, patting them, snug against his heart. He looked and saw Lucas sitting in the boat. The boy was no longer yelling. He looked around confused — and groggy. His head turned in slow motion from side to side.

Grady pushed the canoe out part way and joined the boy in it. "Remember," he said to Karl, "we need a half-hour minimum. Better at 45 minutes."

Karl just stood there, paying no attention to words. He was looking at Lucas.

Suddenly he noticed Grady was waving his hand at Karl and calling his name.

Karl shook himself. "What?"

"We need at least a half-hour. Go finish the job."

Karl nodded.

Ryder pushed hard on the boat, then he jumped in as well. Karl stood there, watching them paddle away. Lucas' eyes stayed on Karl. Karl kept watching until the boat turned, and the boy's eyes were hidden by Grady's back.

Karl knew he would see those eyes forever in his nightmares.

# TWO

Sara Flores felt as happy as she could remember — until she heard the scream. She was paddling a two-person kayak down a lazy part of the Illinois River. The oak trees around the banks had long catkins dripping yellow pollen into the water. They added a painterly touch to the already gorgeous views.

The river meandered left then right, so she never saw far in front. Each bend brought something new. One minute she saw flat fields lush with single-crop plantings. Vistas stretching for a couple of miles. Around the next bend there were woods right up to the river. No visibility beyond them.

The water level was high. She always had to check that before coming — or she'd end up running into sand bars all up and down the stream.

She lifted her face to the deliciously warm sun. In another month, those rays kissing her face would turn into an Oklahoma fireball. But for now it was just perfect.

The smells? Well... some nearby farmer was using cow manure to fertilize his newly-planted crops. It wasn't pleasant. But it was normal outdoor Oklahoma smells, so it was somehow... comforting. Somehow home.

Amazingly, not a single mosquito had shown up. Yet. Sara attracted them in droves. She was Type O blood and she sweated easily — all delicious for mosquitos. She was wearing white because, apparently, the little blood-suckers searched visually for targets and they could more easily see dark colors.

Sara's gray-furred wolf-dog Skidi was riding in the front seat of the kayak. Her co-pilot. Except Skidi wasn't pulling her weight with the rowing.

"You're freeloading up there," she said to Skidi. There was no reply. In fact, Skidi pointedly turned her head away from Sara. Ignoring her.

A two-person kayak took a lot of strength for a single paddler, but they both knew Sara could handle it easily. Enhanced strength comes in handy.

Skidi occupied herself by keeping a sharp yellow eye out for rabbits and other food. She alerted Sara instantly if — horrors — some dog dared to come into her view. Worse if the dog dared to bark at them.

Lately, Skidi liked to stick her head over the side and down into the water. Sara wondered if she was looking for fish. There were enough of them in the river to attract fishermen.

Or maybe Skidi was just dunking her head so she could come up and shake herself — spraying Sara with river water. She had a funny look each time she did it. She'd look at Sara out of the corner of her eye, then she'd snort. Like she was pranking Sara. Then laughing.

Sara grinned.

She turned back to the water and saw it was starting to move a little faster. One of the very mild Type Two rapids was coming up.

Then she heard the scream. High pitched — as if from smaller lungs. A child?

She started paddling downriver as fast as her enhanced strength would let her. And she considered her options. She didn't have a gun with her. It wasn't very practical when kayaking. A gun would need to be in a dry bag to keep it from getting wet. The full minute it would take to open the bag pretty much made it not worth the hassle.

Her available weapons included her Spyderco knife, Skidi, and herself. And surprise — that was her most powerful weapon. No man saw an unarmed woman as a threat.

Sara paddled hard as she considered the scream. Maybe it was in fun? On the rapids? She hoped that was true. But... it hadn't sounded that way.

The water was moving even faster as she turned a bend. On her left, right before the rapids, she saw a small concrete boat launch pad surrounded by woods on both sides. The concrete ran back under a train bridge and disappeared around a corner. Presumably there was a road and parking area hidden back there.

A faded yellow canoe was pulled up and two men were walking away from it — going back under the bridge. The larger one was one holding a small boy.

Sara could see the man's hand over the child's face.

"Hey," she yelled as she paddled faster to them. "Stop!"

They both jerked as though to run but turned their heads back at her. When they saw her, they both stopped. She saw them look at her hands — paddling hard. No gun in them. They looked at each other.

Sara saw them decide. The shorter, wiry one took two steps towards her. He had dark hair, dark eyes and jangly nerves. Like he was plugged into an electric outlet.

"The boy's just throwin a fit," he said. He had a funny, raspy voice. "It's time to go home and he wants to stay."

Sarah used the momentum of her speed to run her kayak up onto the concrete pad, mostly out of the water. She put a smile on her face and got out. She kept her eyes on the man, even as she pulled the kayak the rest of the way from the water. Skidi knew to stay in the boat until Sara called her.

"Kids can be like that," she agreed. "They don't like the word 'no.'"

She looked past the wiry man to the larger one holding the boy. He was an older man, taller, blander somehow. The receding hairline and the extra pounds were a real contrast with the smaller man. The boy he was holding was maybe three years old and very muddy. He was squirming but in a weird way. Like he was in slow motion.

"You don't like the word 'No'?" she asked the kid, walking toward him and the bigger man.

The guy holding the kid frowned at her. "This is not your business, lady."

Sara saw a flash of gray fur in her peripheral vision. She turned and saw Skidi had launched herself at the first guy — grabbing his right arm with her teeth. What the heck? Skidi wouldn't attack without her order. Unless...

The impact knocked the man down, with Skidi landing on top, teeth still holding his arm. Sara saw the hand on that arm was holding a .38 automatic. A Colt?

Sara nodded to herself — *good dog!* Then the man surprised her. He ignored the pain in his right arm and switched the gun over to his left hand.

Sara ran at him to grab the gun. Before she could reach it, he used it to backhand Skidi. Hard. Right on her head.

Sara grabbed his arm with one hand and the gun with the other. But she had eyes only for Skidi, who was now lying on the ground. Limp.

A blinding rage took over Sara. She shoved herself on top of the man, and — using her enhanced strength — started forcing the gun towards the man's chest. He was strong for his size, very strong. But she was stronger. She watched the shock in his eyes as the barrel of the Colt moved closer and closer to his heart.

She was breathing hard, twisting the gun, glaring into his eyes. *But,* she thought, *maybe I should just forget the gun.* What Sara really wanted to do — what she was picturing in her mind — was rip his throat out and chew up his face. And piss on his dead body.

She had just one second to notice another movement in her peripheral vision. Just one second to remember the second man. Just one second to regret being an anger-blinded idiot. And then there was nothing.

# THREE

Sara awoke to confusion. A dream? She was underwater! It was cool and delightful water. Look at the pretty swirls! But... her body was twitching. Twisting. Struggling. Why?

Curious, she saw a bubble leave her mouth and rise, slowly, up.

Air! She couldn't breathe. She *had* to breathe. Why couldn't she breathe? She struggled harder. Desperately harder.

Hands! A man's hands. They were holding her shoulders down under the water.

She grabbed the hands. She couldn't move them! Where was her strength? She twisted. She struggled. She pulled on the hands. She couldn't breathe!

Then there was pain. Was she already dying? No. It was something else. She was confused. She looked at her hands. They were twisting, pulling at the man's hairy arms. His gray-haired, big arms. She was trying to break his hold. She grabbed his fingers to pull them back. But the pain!

At first she didn't understand what she was seeing. She saw hair covering her hands. But not his gray hair — her hands had reddish hair on them. Her hands were *growing* reddish-gray hair? Growing it right before her eyes. No, not hair. Fur!

Her fingernails were growing longer. Harder. They were turning into claws. Her claws were digging into the man's hairy arms — drawing blood. She could see trails and trails of blood floating away in the water. Pretty red swirls.

Then she really panicked.

*Oh, please god, not now!* she begged. She couldn't be transforming to wolf right now. Underwater.

But she was.

Her mind screamed, *But it takes a full minute to transform! I'll drown!*

Now the pain hit harder. All the worst pain of transforming. Her mouth felt like all her teeth were pulled at once — without novocaine. She watched her nose and snout elongate and grow bigger and bigger to her eyes. She felt her spine crack as it turned from a backward curve to a forward curve.

*Skidi!* she remembered. There was something important about Skidi. But it was foggy. So far away.

*So this is how I die,* she thought.

Then she passed out.

# FOUR

The next thing Sara noticed was a different kind of pain. Her left leg was being dragged through shallow water. A rock slammed into her side. Then another. Teeth pulled on her ankle.

"Ow!" she tried to say, but there was something wrong. Her tongue was too long. Her mouth didn't work. And why was someone biting her ankle?

She smelled Skidi.

*Man! Trying to drown her!*

She jerked to full consciousness. But only Skidi was in sight. Skidi, who was dragging her out of the water.

She looked down and saw her body. She was in wolf form.

Sara found she was gulping air. Her throat was raw and her rib cage hurt — both very surprising. The transformation always took away any pain. Why not this time?

Skidi let go of her ankle and ran into the trees by the water. Then she came back and whined. Then returned to the trees.

Sara looked around and saw nobody. But... *Good idea Lassie*, she thought. *Let's get out of the open.* It was not smart to be two wolves out in the open in a state where everyone was packing a gun!

Sara ran into the trees with Skidi, just enough to vanish if anyone came. But where they could still see the river. She looked up it and saw the rapids section. They must have come down the rapids. How did they...?

*Skidi!* Sara moved to her and stuck her snout into Skidi's fur on the back of her head. The skin was broken, and there had been blood. Washed away by the river.

Sara carefully licked Skidi's head wound, rekindling the rage that had overwhelmed her before. She closed her eyes in relief that Skidi was apparently OK. She wanted to transform back to human right now — just so she could wrap Skidi in her arms and reassure herself.

But now wasn't the time. She looked back up the river. She made herself remember it all. Then she sat back on her haunches in aston-ishment.

*How the hell am I even alive?*

Sara didn't know how long she could hold her breath. She'd never needed to know before. But she'd be shocked if it was even a minute. Since she was struggling and fighting at the time — maybe not even a half minute.

She did know that when you passed out, your body gulped for air — automatically. No thinking required.

She should have opened her mouth and sent water rushing into her airways, her lungs. Killing her. Because Skidi sure as heck didn't know how to give her mouth-to-mouth resuscitation. If that was even possible between two canine snouts.

She remembered starting to transform. She remembered her arms turning to paws. Her mouth and nose to a snout. She remembered seeing the man's blood as she clawed his arms. So that was what? Maybe 10-15 seconds into the transformation? She remembered her spine starting to bend.

So how did she not breathe in water and die during the remaining 45 seconds of transforming?

Was there some transformation her throat went through? Her lungs? Did they move when she transformed? She'd never paid them any attention before. She always noticed her hands and her snout turn. She noticed her spine crack because it was the worst of the pain.

She never really paid attention to anything else in the transformation. Why would you be curious about the rest when you spent almost the whole minute wishing you could shoot yourself to make the pain stop?

So the question was... did she normally breathe during those last 45 seconds?

Sara thought back to previous transformations. She was always gulping air right after. No reason for that unless she wasn't breathing during the worst part of it. She'd always assumed she hadn't breathed because of the pain. Maybe she literally *couldn't* breathe during the last part.

Sara shook her head. *Don't go down a rabbit hole with this*, she thought. *Maybe later, but not now.* She stood on all fours and shook her entire body. It felt good. She liked the water flying out in all directions from her coat.

Suspicious, she turned to Skidi. She remembered the way the little brat had splattered water all over her in the kayak. Skidi looked like she was laughing. She smelled amused. And happy. Then Skidi shook herself all over and threw water and sand all over Sara.

*Yes*, Sara had to acknowledge. *Skidi knew exactly what she was doing.*

Sara looked back upriver. She was going to find those two men. And the kid. No matter what.

Sara knew she wasn't especially smart. She'd proved that letting the men beat her. But Sara had one quality stronger than anyone she'd ever met. She was stubborn. She had intervened to save that kid — and if it was at all possible, she would finish the job.

If she got to snack on two evildoers in the process — that would be even better.

She and Skidi swam the river. They kept a nose out for any humans in the area. It was dangerous for two wolves alone in the Oklahoma woods. But Sara needed her wolf nose to check out the men's last location. It took them about a half-hour to reach the boat launch area where the men and the boy had been. Sara put her nose to the ground and deeply inhaled the smells of the two men.

Then she focused on the more elusive smell of the boy. He had been put on the ground at one point. Probably when the bigger man who was holding him clobbered her on the back of her head. The boy had even managed to run a little before the man caught him again.

She had the answer to her first question. The boy was not related to either of the men. They had lied. His blood didn't smell like theirs.

She wasn't sure what it was about blood, but the blood smells of people who were kin to each other had some... flavors?... in common with each other.

It was fun to add a human brain to the results of a wolf nose. Too bad researchers at Yellowstone didn't have a werewolf to advise them! Sara often read their work in an attempt to better understand her new self. The researchers wrote that a wolf pack was more likely to accept a trespasser who was related to them — even if the pack leaders had not yet been born when the trespasser left. So it wasn't a scent *memory* that made the alphas accept them. A werewolf could have explained to them the scent/flavor in the blood that revealed kinship. Maybe she should email them anonymously?

Sara saw Skidi also nosing the boy's scent and the others. Skidi would remember too — which might be critical. In human form, Sara's nose wasn't anywhere near as discerning.

They followed the scent of the threesome to the parking area, where it all disappeared. There were three different treads visible from three different vehicles that had parked there. Sara wanted to remember the treads for the future — but she saw nothing unusual in them. She wasn't sure she could tell the difference between tire treads without something unusual. An embedded nail would have been ideal! Unfortunately...

The men had taken their canoe but left her kayak. She would have expected them to shove the kayak out into the rapids to explain her dead body as a boating accident. But they were probably getting twitchy to get the heck away from the area.

When she and Skidi had learned all they could, Sara ate a squirrel so she could transform back to human. She also congratulated herself for never kayaking without a change of clothes in a dry bag. It would have been very embarrassing — worse memorable! — to arrive naked back at the dock where their truck was waiting.

As always, Sara was relieved to get home. She loved her house. It was an 1100 sq. ft. rectangle with four columns supporting the big overhang on the roof. The size and the tan shingles made it look like most other middle-class Oklahoma homes. But it was surrounded on three sides by a U-curve in the Arkansas River. And the inside was exactly as she wanted it — comfortable, attractive, and protected electronically better than a vault.

Sara stood under her shower until the hot water ran out. She hadn't meant to — she was usually careful about water conservation. But it seemed like she'd just stepped into the water when it turned cold. She had no idea where her mind had gone, but she shook her head to bring it back.

She needed to plan — because nobody gets away with hurting Skidi. Or trying to kill the two of them.

After double-checking Skidi's head and fixing a big slab of steak for each of them, Sara brought a yellow pad, pen and her MacBook to the large comfortable sofa, covered with a Pendleton blanket. Skidi did two circles on her side of it, then collapsed down as though there wasn't a bone in her body. She was quickly asleep.

When the clock turned to 5 PM, Sara clicked on KOTV for the local news. The lead story was about a three-year-old boy named Lucas Johnson missing from the family home near a small town called Smithville — which was right next to the river Sara had been on. The newscast said Lucas has been missing since at least 9:00 this morning. A search of the local area was continuing. There was concern he might have wandered into the forested area to the east.

His parents Noah and Betsy Johnson were on the TV asking for anyone who had seen the boy to please call. They showed a picture that confirmed Sara's suspicion. It was the kid she'd seen — no doubt. But the cops didn't have a clue — they still thought the boy was just missing.

She had no idea how skilled the police were in such a tiny area as Smithville. It was unlikely they had investigated kidnappings before. She knew she needed to alert law enforcement — they could marshal forces she didn't have. With a kidnapping, time was critical.

A quick Internet search told her the FBI could take jurisdiction for kids under 12 who go missing. They didn't have to wait any time period and they didn't need to believe the kid had crossed state lines.

This was good because Sara knew of one good FBI agent in Tulsa. On a previous mission of hers, a large shipment of drugs had left before Sara could stop it. She'd called the FBI and they sent Special Agent Austin Wright from the Tulsa office. He'd stopped the trucks and processed the three dead bodies she'd left behind at the headquarters. She liked how he'd handled the interviews in the aftermath.

There was a minor problem with him, however. He was still looking for the woman who had called it in. For her.

She composed a message that the missing boy had been kidnapped by two men. She gave the time, the river, the boat dock where they'd been parked, and what she remembered about their canoe. And she gave full descriptions of the men.

Then she called her friend Mason Spencer in central Pennsylvania. She'd met Mason when she had to rescue him from a political fixer. The guy wanted to kill Mason because of what Mason found on the fixer's computer.

Mason was one of the very few who knew what she was — since she'd been forced to transform right in front of him. And Mason wanted to join with her. "I want to fight bad guys," he kept telling her. She smiled. She could picture him — his long black hair tied back. His slightly chubby cheeks kept his half Native American heritage from being obvious. His stubborn desire to put his nose into other people's business. Ruefully, she smiled. He was a lot like her in that.

She worried about endangering him. But truthfully, she needed his skills. Like right now.

The first words out of his mouth were, "Are you using the secure phone I sent you?"

"Yes, Mason."

"Good. Then we can talk. You have something for me?"

She told him, "I've got a message that needs to get to a Tulsa FBI agent's inbox and I don't know how to do it safely."

"Sure," he said.

"Mason, this is very dangerous. If he can track it back to you...."

"Won't happen."

"Mason... do you know how many cyber specialists the FBI must have working for them? How many resources they could put into finding you?"

Sara could almost hear him shrugging over the phone. "Well, it's been six months and they haven't found me yet."

Sara was shocked. "You've been inside their system for six months now?"

"Yep."

Sara closed her eyes. The risks he kept taking!

"Sara," he said, as if he were talking to a slow child. "I've gotten a lot better — and a lot more careful — since we met. There are maybe four or five people in the world who could find me now. And I have warning systems on top of warning systems that would alert me in time."

Sara sighed. Maybe it was time to stop treating him like the college kid he used to be. He was a man now. "I can't promise to stop worrying about you," she told him, "because I probably always will. But I'll try to stop questioning your abilities."

"You'll use me more now?"

"Yes. And I'll have to start paying you too. Maybe I'll let you look into the hidden accounts of the next rich murderer who bites the dust. We can split it."

She could picture his grin. She dictated the message to him, then hung up. She had a grin of her own.

Sara got up and went to the fridge for her "guilty pleasure," a Diet Coke. Yes, she knew cola drinks were loaded with chemicals that could dissolve teeth in just a day or two and do who knew what all else. Maybe when she transformed, her body not only healed bullet holes — but also chemical damage?

Sara hoped so. Because in the late afternoon Sara had found nothing else jolted your brain awake like Diet Coke. She even liked the feeling of it burning her mouth and throat on the way down.

Skidi was looking at her when she sat back down on the sofa with the can.

"I know, I know," Sara told her.

While the FBI was (hopefully!) searching for the two men through databases and manpower — Sara wanted to focus on their smell to find them. She started by admitting she'd never find them if they were strangers who happened upon the kid by chance and decided to take him. Maybe there were child kidnap rings who delivered kids to order? Someone decides they want a nice little blond boy three years old and they're willing to pay a fortune? No questions asked?

But no. Not in this case. Such men, if they exist, wouldn't be looking for a specific type of kid in a tiny town in the middle of nowhere. They'd be looking where there were lots of kids and lots of confusion. So, really, there were only two possibilities she could see. Either that chance happening or... someone who knows the kid decided to take him.

A parent — Sara had read about that happening. But both the boy's parents were on TV looking frantic. One of them could be faking, of course. *Was I always this cynical?* she wondered. *Or am I just seeing too many evil people lately? Maybe I'll end up with those dead eyes you see in some cops.*

Sara shook her head. She was retracing old thoughts. If she wasn't using her powers to rescue people — what else was there? Scaring the pants off kids at birthday parties?

She returned to her analysis. It could be a parent. Or... she'd read about a nanny who helped kidnap one of her charges. There probably aren't any nannies in Smithville, but there could be babysitters — looking for a payday. But it would be a risk — a young girl would be more likely to regret it and talk.

So, she decided. A parent, an adult relative, or a neighbor.

She looked at her watch. Time to call Mason again. And fuel up more. She needed to arrive in Smithville about 11 tonight. She'd heard farmers and ranchers get up very, very early. Eleven PM would give her four to five hours of safe-ish search time.

Mason had found three relatives in Smithville — the wife's brother and two grown children belonging to the husband from a first marriage. Mason complained to her that Facebook was a little harder to penetrate than the FBI, but he'd managed.

"Just FYI," he said as she was about to hang up. "I gave you a code name in the email to FBI agent Wright."

"You did what?"

"You might want to use him again, so he needs to know a message from you is reliable."

"I hesitate to ask what you named me?"

"Truth Teller."

Sara thought about it. "That's actually pretty good. Thank you!"

Sara found the addresses on her map for the three relatives and marked them. She's already marked the Johnson family house.

# FIVE

.

Smithville was about an hour from her home. Other than the tiny town, the whole area showed on Google Maps as woodland dotted here and there on the edges by the occasional ranch house or farmhouse.

Sara drove her three-year-old F-150 down a road that butted up to a big track of the woods. She found a spot where the side of the road was smooth and pulled the truck off onto it. She put a torn piece of cardboard on the dash, showing through the front window. It said, "Back tomorrow AM with tow truck."

She took off her clothes and put them in the small matte-black, waterproof backpack that fit her wolf body. She added her Rugar LC9 with one extra magazine and her Spyderco knife.

She had long ago removed the bulb from the interior light, so all stayed dark when she opened the door and got out with Skidi. She sighed deeply and gritted her teeth. No putting it off. She hated the pain of the transformation. Every time she was about to do it she swore to herself it would be the last time. But somehow — maybe she had masochistic tendencies? — she kept doing it.

"It's only a minute," she whispered, closing her eyes and grimacing. "I can take it."

And she did.

She had laid the bag on the ground on its end, with the arm straps in perfect position to put paws through. She nosed her snout under the bag and shrugged it onto her back. It was awkward because she couldn't fasten a clasp to hold it. She'd tried and tried but failed. She could open a clasp while in wolf form. She just needed to slip her bottom jaw under it and position one fang on the clasp. It worked every time. But she'd not yet found a way to fasten it.

She and Skidi quickly moved into the woods. It was the typical oak and pine tree forest seen in this area, with some hickory thrown in. The low brush on the forest floor wasn't too deep.

About a mile from the parked car, they found a spot to leave the bag. It was a shallow depression, and there was a decent-sized rock nearby to put on top. She shrugged off the bag, dumped it in the hole and then pushed the rock over it.

Then she and Skidi peed on the ground around it. She wanted to make very sure they could find it fast — in case they were in a big hurry.

Sara took big gulping breaths of night air in the woods. Of freedom. She wanted to... heck why not? She flopped down on the leaves and rolled over. She wiggled her butt and let the ground scratch her back. It kicked up delicious smells. Leaf mold. Animal droppings. The passage of worms. Life. And a good friend — because Skidi was rolling in the leaves right beside her.

Reluctantly, she got back up. Time to work.

It was about five miles to the family home — staying in the forest. They only left cover once when they had a dirt road with no traffic to cross. They could have cut the time in half if they were willing to cross tall grass prairie — and be visible to anyone looking.

Sara kept an easy trot, pushing it just a little, and they arrived in the woods surrounding the Johnson family ranch in about an hour. Sara saw in front of her the two back buildings she'd seen on Google

Maps. Assuming the large one held animals, she had come in from the opposite side of the house. And they had some luck. There was a small breeze coming right at them, so their scent shouldn't carry. Sara found sheep got a little crazy at her scent — she couldn't imagine why(!) And the family was likely to have at least one dog.

The house itself had started as a plain rectangular box with vinyl siding on it. Another rectangle had been added at some point — making an "L" shape. There was a big front porch with an open door into the living room — the screen door all that was keeping out the bugs. There was a single, warm light on in that room and another showing from a further back room — Sara guessed the kitchen. A low murmur came from the front room — two people were talking in a low voice.

She and Skidi moved closer — but stayed at least 25 feet away. Sara had learned (thank you, Google!) that almost all motion detectors linked to outdoor lights cut off about 20 feet away. Only a very few had a range out to 60 feet. A farm or ranch was unlikely to pay for the added distance — or even want it. Given roving wildlife, such a light would be going on and off all night.

Sara was also careful to stay downwind.

She sniffed the air. She could smell six people in the room — three men and two women — no... one woman and one girl. The girl was older than the missing boy — she was menstruating. She had to be the boy's sister — she smelled of his same flavor. The girl and two of the men were sleeping — she could hear their slow breathing.

There were three trucks and one police car parked on the dirt drive. Sara moved to check them out. The police car had many smells — oil, gas, gun powder, stale fast food. But she also recognized the smell of one of the sleeping men inside. He had no kin smells to the family.

She checked out the trucks. One was driven primarily by the woman — who had to be Betsy Johnson. The second truck smelled mostly of the second sleeping man. She analyzed his scent. He smelled nothing like the woman but had a kin smell to the girl in the house and the missing boy. So he was the father — Noah Johnson.

The third truck smelled primarily of the man who was talking to the mother. Something in his smell... it was similar to the mother's. Mason had found three nearby relatives. Two were related to the father and one to the mother. So the man talking to Betsy must be her brother Karl Nilsson.

Sara moved to where she could see inside the house.

Suddenly the room erupted in a cascade of yipping. A white fluffy lapdog was straining at the screen door — standing on her paws and barking her little head off.

They were busted.

Sara raised her paw to hand-signal Skidi to stay there, then she disappeared around the side of the closest barn.

She was too big to pass for a dog, at 130 pounds. But Skidi was half dog and just 100 pounds. It was important for the family to see a dog to explain the barking. If they thought prowler or wolf, they might come with guns.

Sara heard the woman's, "What are you barking at?" at the door. Then Sara gave Skidi the paw signal to come to her.

"It's just a dog," she heard the policeman say, sounding like he just woke up. "But... good time to take a walk around the house."

"I'll join you," said the father.

It was easy for Sara and Skidi to hide outside the flashlight range and still get good smells from the two men. The cop was very young — this was likely his first job. He smelled concerned. Worried. Tired. Afraid of how this might turn out. Pretty much what she would expect.

The husband was older — maybe mid-30s. Smallish and thin. Handsome in that Oklahoma male look — scrubbed clean with buzz-cut hair under an always-there cowboy hat. Only the shine was off now. He smelled of anguish. Grief. Fear. Sara could detect no false note from him — either in his smell or the tone of his voice.

Finally, the men returned to the house. Sara and Skidi came back in closer.

The third man — probably her brother Karl — was at the door saying goodbye. He looked Scandinavian — blonde hair prematurely turning grey on his mustache and goatee. Blue eyes — which Sara could see perfectly well with her wolf eyes. Fortunately, wolves and dogs are not color blind, despite what you sometimes read. They can see blues and yellows just fine — but not reds.

Betsy Johnson was at the door with her brother. She was a tiny thing, also Scandinavian. With her long blonde hair, she would have been girlie pretty — if her eyes weren't puffy and red. "You go home," she said to Karl Nilsson. "Get some rest. I'll call you the minute we hear anything."

"You hold on," he said to her. "I'm sure we'll find him soon. I'll be back in the morning."

He started to leave, then he came back and took her in his arms and hugged her. "Betsy, I'm so sorry you have to go through this!"

"I'm so scared," she said into his shoulder. Then she pulled back and took a deep breath. She turned him around and pushed him further out the door.

"Go now," she said, "or I'll start crying again."

Karl walked to his Chevy Silverado and got in. Back in the doorway, Noah Johnson put his arm around Betsy and walked her back into the house.

Karl Nilsson rolled down his window and stared at the house for a minute. Then he started the truck and drove off. Leaving a stench of guilt floating in the air behind him.

Sara watched him go, then nodded at Skidi. They ran back through the woods towards her car, carefully re-crossed the road, and ran some more. When they were almost to where she'd cached her backpack, Skidi nosed up some kind of ground rodent and caught it in her teeth — enough to hold it but not kill it. Sara didn't know if it was a mole or gopher or whatever — and she didn't want to know. It was bad enough she had to eat it.

Sara had seen online chat rooms where people talk about how fantastic it would be to be a werewolf. They seemed to find it glamorous. Sara thought those people might think differently if they knew you had to eat meat in order to transform back to human. And — if you're away from your house — you can't just walk up to a McDonald's for that meat.

Skidi waited until Sara nodded her snout, then Skidi swung her head and tossed the animal up in the air. Sara caught it, closed her eyes, and devoured it. Then she lay down and let the pain of the transformation take her.

They were only a couple hundred feet from her clothes stash, but it seemed like the forest floor was composed of one sharp rock after another. All of which her bare human feet seemed to find.

"Yeah, this is really glamorous," she muttered to Skidi. There was a funny feeling in her mouth. She reached in and removed something caught on a tooth. It felt like... fur?

"Is this rodent fur?" she asked Skidi. "Really? Eww. Gak!" She tossed it as far as she could.

Sara recovered her backpack and put her clothes — and shoes — back on. Then she noticed Skidi prancing.

"Are you laughing at me?" she asked.

Skidi didn't answer, but she danced even more around Sara.

"You think it's funny, don't you? You little brat!"

They walked towards where the car was parked. Sara continued the conversation. "I don't see you eating these rodents. You're waiting for a nice steak at home, aren't you?"

Skidi thought it was a great game and rang circles around her.

Sara shook her head and smiled. "I'd rather wait for steak myself. If I could just figure out how to drive in wolf form!"

She smiled wider. "And wouldn't that be a sight for a passing car!"

It was one-thirty in the morning when they parked on the side of a different road. The map said the turnoff to Nilsson's road was two miles ahead. It was another mile after that turnoff to get to his house. Sara didn't want her truck any closer.

She stretched and patted her pockets. She made sure she had her phone, her Rugar LC9 and her Spyderco knife — plus a few extras that might come in handy.

She started a fast jog down the road with Skidi running at her side. She watched for car lights that would require them to jump off the road and flatten themselves in the brush.

Sara had despised jogging her entire life. Boring. Pointless. And did she mention — boring? But now, she actually liked it. The difference was it felt really good. As soon as she hit a certain rhythm, her body started humming. Almost singing. Like it was more natural for her than walking. Maybe it was more natural — for the wolf part of her. The body just chugged away and she could use her mind to feel the world.

She listened to the sounds of the night. The animals. The leaves rustling in the light breeze that was now kissing her face. The smells. She wasn't *in* the night. She *was* the night.

Almost too soon, they arrived at Karl Nilsson's house. It was dark, but Sara could still see. It was a farmhouse, shingled, with a full wraparound porch. She could see it had once been grand — like it wanted to be the main house for a successful family clan. Now, however, it wasn't being kept up. She saw peeling paint on the shutters. Weeds. Signs of a place kept by a single man living alone. A little sad and forgotten.

There was only one vehicle in the drive — the Chevy Silverado.

Sara kept Skidi near her as she circled the house, keeping 25 feet away. Given the state of disrepair, she doubted Karl would have sprung for more powerful light sensors.

She strained, but she heard nothing. Time to get closer. She moved to a side of the house where there were two larger windows and a smaller bath window — both behind the porch. There were no doors on this side.

Sara picked up a small rock from the ground and showed it to Skidi.

"Fetch," she said and threw the rock to within about 3 feet of the veranda. Skidi dashed after the rock and came trotting proudly back with it. She dropped it at Sara's feet. It was undoubtedly the very rock she threw — Sara had given up trying to test her long ago. What came back was always the same size and shape as what she threw — no matter how far she threw it.

What was important now is that no floodlights went on from Skidi's trip.

Sara patted her side, which told Skidi to stay right beside her. Then she walked to the veranda, taking the path Skidi had previously. She squatted low in front and listened hard. She could hear footsteps in the room on her left. Probably a living room or den. Mostly muffled. Occasionally not.

If she had to bet, it sounded like one man. Pacing. Sara strained her ears to find any other sounds. Any other person. She heard none, but if they were in another room she might not.

She looked carefully at the veranda. It wasn't as deep here on the side as it was on the front and the back. Maybe five feet wide. Just room for the two plastic chairs, side by side. She saw no miniature electronic boxes up high, looking down.

She stood and put her hands on the railing, then vaulted herself over — as quietly as she could. She squatted down, raised a hand to stay Skidi, and waited. Nothing happened.

She stood. She looked at Skidi and put her finger to her lips. Then she waved both palms up towards her chest.

Skidi leapt up into her arms. She always staggered Sara when she did that, but it was quiet. No dog nails scratching on the decking. Sara put her down.

She moved along the house side, staying away from the windows. She put her ear against the siding and listened more. Near the front, near the back, near the bathroom. No sounds, other than Nilsson in the front room pacing.

Time to make a move.

Just then, from the front room, Sara heard the sound of chimes — the preset sound from an iPhone ringing.

"What took you so long?" she heard Nilsson ask. "I've been waiting."

Sara couldn't hear the reply. Even wolf ears had their limits.

"I know. I won't call again. But... just tell me the boy's alright. And far away from here."

Silence.

"Yes, I got the deed and the IOUs. So we're clear, right?"

A very long silence.

"Thank you... but that isn't necessary." Nilsson sounded very hesitant.

After a short pause, he said, "Well... OK. Ten grand would be a nice bonus. When is he coming? Now? OK, well, thanks." Nilsson hung up and walked out of the room.

Sara heard a car coming down the driveway. She heard it pull up to the front of the house.

Inside the house, she heard the unmistakable sound of a shotgun racking.

From the front, she heard a car door open and someone step out. Booted feet went up the stairs and there was a knock on the front door.

"Yes," came Nilsson's voice from inside.

"It's Ryder. I got your delivery here." The voice outside was rough. Raspy. Familiar?

"Just leave it by the door. Thanks."

"No can do — boss wouldn't like it."

"OK," said Nilsson, with a funny note in his voice.

Sara heard the door open, then she heard gunfire. A large caliber pistol shot almost simultaneous with a shotgun firing. Then two more pistol shots.

Then silence.

Sara had drawn her gun when the first shot was fired. Now she reminded herself, *You can't kill them. You need them to find the boy.*

The problem with that was neither of them would have the same compunction about killing her.

Sara moved to the corner and peeked around. Nothing. She moved quietly to the door, gun held in both hands just below her eye level. A quick glimpse in the door showed a short, wiry man bending over Nilsson, searching his pockets. Arm shots were too easy to miss with the slightest movement, so she fired a shot into his right thigh — carefully away from the femoral artery.

She gave Skidi a particular sign even before the man started to turn, and Skidi raced in and clamped her jaws around the man's wrist — the one holding the gun. It was the "capture" sign, not the "kill" sign, so Skidi held the wrist tight enough to prevent movement — but didn't snap close her jaws.

The combination of a collapsing leg and Skidi's weight sent the man down to the floor beside Nilsson.

Sara saw his face. The whole thing was deja vu. It was the kidnapper Skidi had attacked before. She remembered him switching hands with the gun — and knocking out Skidi!

Sara ran to him and grabbed at the gun. The man — Ryder apparently — squeezed his grip and held on. Skidi also held on.

Sara tried to tamp down her rage. She put her face next to the man. In a very low voice, she said, "You hurt my wolf. You tried to kill me. I *really* want to tell her to bite off your hand."

He glared at her for a moment. Then he let go. She pocketed the gun.

She kicked the shotgun away from Nilsson and toed him. She was reasonably sure he was dead. His shirt was coated with blood over his heart — and there was no blood still moving. Keeping her gun pointed at Ryder, Sara checked Nilsson's throat for a pulse just to be safe. There wasn't one.

She told Ryder, "Use your jacket to stop your leg bleeding."

He did it. Then he looked at her and said, "You better run, girlie. 'Cause when my boss finds you...."

Sara grinned. "Ooh, I'm just *so* scared!"

It was not the response Ryder expected.

Sara moved to the opposite side of him from Skidi. She grabbed his free arm and pinched hard — right where the ulnar nerve was. While he was screaming, she rolled the man over on top of the arm Skidi was still holding.

She knelt on his back and grabbed a heavy-duty zip tie from her pocket — one of the action goodies she always took with her. She jerked his good hand hard up his back. She reached under him and grabbed the wrist Skidi still had in her mouth.

She nodded at the dog, who released it to her. Skidi kept her head near the man and started a slow, menacing growl. Her jaws were just inches from his eyes.

While he watched Skidi, Sara twisted that arm back to join the other and fastened both wrists in a zip tie. Tight — but not so tight she'd have to loosen it periodically. She took a moment to check his hands. There was no gray hair on them and no deep claw marks. So it had been the other man who tried to drown her.

Sara searched Ryder. In addition to the .380 Colt Government model he'd been holding, Ryder also had a snub nose .22 Taurus in his boot, zip ties of his own, brass knuckles and the Blood Moon Bowie knife — the one considered scariest looking of all the knives.

He had a wallet with a couple hundred dollars and a driver's license in it. Nothing else. The license said he was Ryder Williams, living in Tulsa. She pulled out her phone and texted Mason the man's name and license information. Most important — she found a cell phone. It would be good for the FBI — they could probably track his calls.

She grabbed Ryder's shoulders and dragged him to a plain wall. She pulled him up to a sitting position against it, his hands undoubtedly painful behind his back.

She went back and searched Nilsson's body. Another cell phone for the FBI — the last call he received would be valuable. No additional weapons on him except for a pocket knife.

Although her nose told her nobody else was in the house, she searched it. It was big and mostly unused. There were rooms with thick dust on the furniture — rooms she figured hadn't been used in years. After finding nobody and after sneezing away the dust she'd stirred up, she put Skidi on house guard duty to make sure nobody else arrived while she was distracted.

Finally she grabbed a sofa cushion and plopped it down on the floor right beside the man. She sat down on it next to his legs and zip-tied them together.

His eyes kept moving from Skidi to her. She looked into his eyes and inhaled his scent. Some fear of her. Some embarrassment she took him. A whole lot of anger. Worry too — probably about his boss.

"Here's how it's going to go," she told him. "We need to find the boy — Lucas Johnson — as quick as we can. So you're going to give us the full details — while I film you with my cell phone."

He looked in horror at her cell phone. "The hell with you, lady!"

"Well," she said in her most reasonable voice, "there you're wrong. I'm not a lady. When I look at you, I see a disgusting piece of shit who kills for money and who's perfectly fine with kidnapping small kids. So my preference would be for you to die very, very slowly in as much pain as possible."

She stared at him, letting her rage show. "For what you did to my wolf here, I'd like to strangle you myself. So I'm kind of hoping you don't talk right away."

The man looked away and mumbled. But she heard him.

"You can't?"

He nodded. "I can't."

"Because of your boss?"

He nodded. "You just don't know…"

"Your boss is nothing compared to me."

The man scoffed.

Sara's phone dinged. She looked at it. "Looks like your boss isn't as smart as you think. Your driver's license is real. Or maybe he planned for you to be expendable?"

Ryder said nothing.

"Where is Lucas Johnson?"

Ryder's head was hanging down and he was shaking it from side to side.

Sara slapped him, hard.

"Look at me," she said. "I'm your worst nightmare. You never even dreamed there was something as bad as me in the world."

The man rolled his eyes. Sara patted him on the cheek with her right hand. She kept patting him as her hand transformed to paw — with claws. She kept patting him, now just with her claws. She dragged one of them down his cheek, leaving a trail of blood.

He flinched away slightly and looked at her hand. He saw something that obviously could not be there.

He blinked his eyes rapidly and looked again. Then he jerked his head back as far away from her paw as he could get. His eyes fixed on her paw as if willing the sight to change. He blinked hard, hoping what he saw would change. But it didn't. He stared hardest at where her paw became a human arm.

Slowly he turned his very wide eyes to her face.

"Grady's hands were all scratched up," he said, remembering. "Claw marks."

"Exactly," she said. "So, Grady? Good to know his name. But, focus Ryder. A few claw marks are nothing compared to the rest. Here's the main show."

His head was back against the wall — as far as it would go. Sara moved her face to six inches from his. Then she started the transformation to her face.

Slowly, as slowly as she could, her nose, mouth and chin started joining. Becoming one snout. At the same time, they started elongating. Moving closer and closer to Ryder's face.

He jerked his head to the left. She moved her face left. He jerked his face to the right. She followed.

Eventually Ryder stopped and just watched.

Sara had guesstimated the distance perfectly. When her snout was fully formed, it just touched the man's nose.

He shivered.

He scrunched his eyes tightly closed.

She didn't move.

He lasted for maybe a second, then opened them wide again.

For the finale, Sara started to open her jaws. Slowly. Half inch by half inch. Teeth were exposed. A *lot* of teeth! Forty-two of them on display. Gleaming white and very, very sharp. Right in Ryder's face. Front and center in his vision were four very sharp, very big canine teeth. Almost three inches long.

When her jaw opened to its max, Sara put her two bottom canines under Ryder's chin and stretched to put her two top canines on his forehead.

His eyes rolled up and he slumped down on the bottom canines. She barely managed to back off in time without puncturing his face.

*OK*, Sara thought. *Lesson learned. I wanted to be terrifying, but not enough for him to pass out.*

Frustrated, Sara got up and went to the kitchen. She filled a pan with cold water from the faucet and came back. She threw the water in Ryder's face. Time was wasting. She couldn't interrogate him until she had a human mouth, and she couldn't transform her face back right now. Because if he woke up and saw her as human — he'd never believe it was real.

Ryder sputtered and jerked and came awake. His eyes focused on her. Wolf snout on a human body.

"Oh god," he mumbled. "Oh god, oh god, oh god."

Sara moved her cushion back about two feet and sat down on it again.

She took out her cell phone and transformed her face back to human. She set the phone to record.

# SIX

FBI Special Agent Austin Wright was jolted out of a weird dream. He was somehow a rodeo cowboy who was lassoing one criminal after another. In a rodeo ring. To the cheers of the crowd.

He shook his head and reached blindly for his cellphone, which was charging on his bedside table. Whenever he woke like this, it was almost always a ding from his cell telling him he had a text.

The phone showed five in the morning. He stifled a groan so as not to wake Amelia. They'd both had a late night because Bobby was teething.

He saw a text from Truth Teller. He'd set his office phone to forward anything from the guy. It said, "Read your email. You can save Lucas Johnson if you act fast."

Austin got up fast and hurried to his den — really their small third bedroom, which he'd commandeered for a home office. He logged in securely and found an email with a video attachment. He forwarded the email to Tech — to try to find the source. Although they had not had success with the previous email.

He played the video. After three minutes, he paused it and called their office in Little Rock, Arkansas. He got the SAC (Special Agent in Charge) and got a team moving to the address given in the video. Then he watched the rest.

He called a backup team to join him and another to start watching a particular house in Tulsa. Orders were to let nobody leave it. Then he threw on some clothes, jumped in his three-year-old Honda CRV, and drove to Smithville.

As he drove, he ran the video again through in his mind. He'd never seen anything like it before. The guy — Ryder Williams — told everything — names, locations, crimes committed. He gave up the man who ordered the kidnapping. He talked fast and he looked terrified.

The email accompanying the video said the man was tied up in Karl Nilsson's house, address given in Smithville. It said he was waiting there for the FBI to pick him up — along with his and Karl Nilsson's cell phones. It said Ryder had a gunshot leg wound received while he was killing Nilsson.

In the video this Ryder Williams was all wet — face and clothes. But there hadn't been any rain in these parts in a couple of weeks. Austin had a terrible thought — had the man been waterboarded? It would explain his terror and how wet he was.

But... Austin had seen waterboarding once. That man had talked, but not like this man did. Not all alert and eager to... to... it seemed like Williams wanted to please someone. Desperately.

And... who was taking the video? Austin was looking forward to perhaps an eye witness to this "Truth Teller."

# SEVEN

Five hours later, Special Agent Austin Wright should have been happy. He had the kid safe. He had both of the actual kidnappers and a full confession from one of them. He had the man who'd ordered it in custody. Win. Win. Win.

Instead, Austin wanted to put his fist through the wall. Ryder Williams sat in front of him in their puke green Interview A room. He was on a cheap metal chair, leg bandaged and drinking coffee. He had just finished re-telling everything from the video for their hidden camera. He was even eager to tell everything. But it wasn't making any real sense.

Austin took a deep breath and let it out slowly.

"Let's go over this again," he said.

Williams nodded. "Sure. OK. But tell me first — didya get the boy? Was he still at the address I gave you?"

Austin nodded. "He's safe. His family is on their way to get him."

"Good. Good." Williams nodded some more and took another sip of his coffee.

"Mr. Williams, help me understand. If you care about the boy, why were you involved in kidnapping him?"

"See, that's what I've been trying to tell you. That was the old me. I didn't usedta think about anybody but myself."

"And the reason for this change to the new you?"

"I think the kid must have been sorta like the last straw. After we took him, I realized I couldn't do it no more. I had to change."

"So you went to Karl Nilsson's house with a gun?"

Williams's eyes darted left then right. Then he looked right back at Austin.

"I figured I'd bring him in when I talked. Maybe get some consideration from you guys. Ya know?"

"But you entered with your gun out?"

"Well, yeah. I ain't runnin' into some house without my gun. And he had a shotgun! He fired at me and I fired at him. That's like self-defense!"

"And the double-tap to his head after?"

"See, that's whatchacall instinct — I did it without thinking. After, that's when I decided to come clean. Change my life."

"Who took the video of you?"

Williams clenched his lips together and shook his head no.

"Were you threatened?"

Williams got the strangest look in his eyes and made a noise almost like a snort. Then he said, "You got my statement. That's all I got to say." Then he laid his head down on the table.

Austin just didn't buy it. He said, "If you were threatened, just tell me and we can protect you."

The head didn't move, but Austin heard another snort.

Fumbling for anything, Austin said, "We could get you a psychiatrist to talk to. Anything you told them...."

Williams head shot up. He said "No!" He stared at Austin to make sure his "no" was understood. He even repeated it. Then he laid his head back down on the table.

Austin sat there dumbfounded. He'd seen absolute terror in the man's eyes. For a psychiatrist?

He wanted to get to the bottom of this. He wanted to uncover this

"Truth Teller." But he could just hear what his boss would say. "You got the kid back. You got all the perps and a confession. It's a big win and you want to pick at it? Meanwhile — you've got how many unsolved cases?"

He could picture himself saying to his boss, "But this Truth Teller. There's something wrong with him."

No, he didn't think for a minute this "Truth Teller" was involved in the kidnapping. All the tips were to stop the plot. What really worried him was this "Truth Teller" seemed very close to a vigilante. Right here, in Tulsa, Oklahoma. Austin saw big future trouble coming from this guy.

Ryder's head stayed down. Finally Austin stood up. Future problems were for the future. For now he had plenty of other cases to solve. He said, "We'll get your statement printed for you to sign, then you can go back to your cell."

Ryder Williams was barely listening. He finally heard the door close and he sighed in relief. Alone, he reran in his mind what the bitch had told him after she finished recording him. After she sent the video to somebody.

"Listen to me now, Ryder, because this is very important. Your whole future depends on it."

He'd looked up. He was already thinking about how he could get out of the recording. Duress, wasn't that what they said? Something you say under duress can't count.

"You're thinking how you can get out of this, right?"

He just looked at her.

"But you really, really don't want to. If you accept this, you could go away for kidnapping — but you should get a reduced sentence for cooperating with the FBI. Identifying the others involved. Helping them rescue the kid."

She nodded over at Karl's body. "You could probably even get away with self-defense for him. You'll do time, but you'll get out when you're still young enough to enjoy it. You could even come after me when you're out — if you're dumb enough to try it. Point is, you'll have choices. All you have to do is stick with what you said on the tape — but give them nothing else.

"Or..." she said, staring at him. "You could make a very bad decision. You could tell them about me. Anything about me. They're going to push you hard. They will really want to know who was holding the camera. But they don't need to know that to finish the case — it'll just be cop curiosity. They'll give up on it eventually.

"But suppose you tell them I'm a werewolf. Everyone knows werewolves aren't real. Picture yourself telling them that." She laughed. "Can you imagine it?"

She waited. "What would happen? You'll get yourself committed to a mental hospital. Nobody will ever believe you. And getting committed to a mental hospital is the very worst thing that could happen to you.

"Why? Because I can easily get to you in a hospital. They're desperate for hospital workers. There's any number of jobs I could fill. You are completely — totally — helpless in a mental hospital. I can get to you and get back out again. It's not like if you're in prison.

"You keep your mouth completely shut about me, and I'll leave you alone. You can still have a life. You mention me at all and you'll be sent to a psych ward, and I will come for you. You'll be helpless to stop me.

"You know wolves love meat, right? We like to gorge on it. Lucky for you I'd just eaten a big meal before coming here. But even so, when I had your head in my jaws — it was really, really hard not to bite down. Rip a chunk off of you.

"I wonder sometimes how many chunks you could rip off a person and eat — before they died. I'm thinking maybe a hundred. Or more. With you — it would be very satisfying to try."

She turned to the wolf at her side. "What do you think, Jane? Would it be fun?"

That wolf walked right up to Ryder and stared at him. Then she growled. Showed her teeth.

The woman stood up. She smiled her most unnerving smile. "You didn't think I was the only one, did you? There are lots of us. Probably close to a thousand in the United States alone. Some of us work as nurses — you'll want to especially remember that. I know two who have clerical positions in the FBI. So I'll know what you tell them."

She and the wolf walked to the door. She turned back to Ryder. "Don't try to invent some story about me — they'll trip you up. Just say absolutely nothing — and you'll still have a life.

"And Jane and I will have to find somebody else to snack on."

She stuck out her tongue and ran it all around her mouth. The wolf's tongue was also hanging out. Then the woman waved bye, and they left.

Ryder shuddered. He'd keep his mouth shut — as long as he was trapped in a prison. And he'd stay far away from any hospital.

But... when he got out, he could get her. Maybe. He'd have to think about that. Now that he knew what kind of freak he was dealing with — he could think up a plan. He was pretty sure he'd read silver could kill them. He'd have time to come up with a really good plan.

# EIGHT

About that same time, Sara was back home, relaxing on her sofa and scratching Skidi's back.

"A thousand werewolves just in the U.S.," she said and laughed. "I'll have to remember that for the next person to scare." She shook her head. "I don't think I'd like that many of us running around. But it's lonely being the only one.

"Or am I? Surely there must be others? Maybe it's time for me to try to find out? What do you think?"

Skidi always chuffed her agreement to Sara's questions — but not this time. She just looked at Sara, hard. Then she closed her eyes and stretched under Sara's scratching.

Sara watched her, considering.

"You may be right," she said. "There's a whole lot of ways finding another werewolf could go really, really bad."

END

Author of *The Stench of Fear* and *Curiosity Kills*

# SUE DENVER

"It's like Jack Reacher and Jane Yellowrock parented a kid who can use either a gun or fangs to take out bad guys."
-MJ Silversmith, *Discovery*

# Amateur Assassin

A WolfLady™ Mystery Novella

# ONE

Amateur Assassin
By Sue Denver

Werewolf Sara Flores was sitting on the New York City 4-train, heading to where she could catch the Staten Island Ferry and see the Statue of Liberty from the water. It was number one on her to-do list for her first vacation in over a year.

She was *not* in rural Oklahoma anymore — the sensory cacophony was astonishing. Her ears were probably leaking blood from the high, loud screams of the train brakes, and she for-sure had a bruise on her shoulder from slamming into a pole when she first boarded. She realized riding the subway was like being in a bumper car, and she had to either sit down or hang on tight to something.

And then there was her nose...

The nose overload started on the airplane here. She'd been seated next to someone who needed lessons in how to wipe his butt. While all smells were wonderful when she was in wolf form, some were really disgusting in her human form.

There was some of that on this subway car — a hint to her right of urine and beyond that a few molecules of days-old vomit. All cleaned up probably good enough for strictly human noses.

There was fun for her nose here as well. She was currently sorting the passengers into meat-eater and vegetarian and further sorting the meat-eaters into those who liked spices in the meat instead of the plain steak-and-potatoes smells of most Oklahomans.

The breaks screamed as the car jolted to a stop. Two people stood up and left the train. Just one person entered the car, but Sara's head jerked to the short black woman as if pulled by a magnet.

The woman was reeking of fear.

Nothing — absolutely nothing — captured the attention of Sara's wolf as did fear.

The woman looked like she might turn and run at any second. Instead she moved into the car and sat at a seat across from and about 25 feet away from Sara. She lowered her head, but her eyes were darting left and right — furtively. Like she didn't want to attract attention, but she wanted to memorize everything she saw.

She was very tiny — no more than 5' tall. Attractive. Sara couldn't guess her age well — she was maybe in her 40s. Her hair was natural and floated around her face.

Sara's wolf found her fascinating.

The woman was very skinny — but not fashionably so. Skinny like she didn't get enough to eat. Like it was affecting her health.

Maybe that was why her clothes didn't fit her very well? She was dressed the same as some other women in the car. She had a long skirt that covered some unusual-looking sneakers. A light jacket — appropriate for the early October weather.

The clothes were worn — but not worn into her body. Like someone else had worn them until recently.

Her fear was like catnip to Sara's wolf.

Before she could stop herself, Sara stood. She grabbed onto the metal bar that ran the length of the car to steady herself from the swaying motion. Using the bar, she walked — casually, she hoped — towards the woman, dodging other "strap hangers."

The train made a jerking turn, and she nearly fell into the lap of a young male school kid with pimples and a huge backpack sitting at his feet. He was somewhere inside his head, eyes glazed over, and didn't even notice her.

Finally, she stumbled past Mystery Woman and up to a schematic of subway train routes on the wall. She traced her finger along the route they were traveling — to explain why she'd moved. And she inhaled through her nose.

The fear was strong, but there was another scent she'd missed before. More subtle. Something, not fear. Something like determination — or resolve. Sara looked at her from the corner of her eyes.

The woman's teeth were clenched, and her face... was interesting. Her head was down and her shoulders hunched in on herself — all signs of fear and trying to blend into the woodwork. But her eyes didn't match the rest of the body language. They were checking out everything. Assessing everything. As her eyes moved towards Sara, Sara faced her eyes forward on the map. She carefully did not move her eyes to the woman — but only used her peripheral vision. She saw the mystery woman's eyes stop on her. Pause. Evaluate. Then move on.

They were almost like cop eyes!

Sara turned back and returned to her seat, taking another deep scent-breath as she passed the woman. She found yet another mystery to the woman — her you-are-what-you-eat smell. It was different from any of the other passengers. She didn't smell like a meat-eater or a vegetarian. What the heck was this woman eating?

Once seated again, Sara considered. A woman who's both afraid and determined. Could she be a terrorist? That would make sense — but there was no smell of explosives.

Sara knew the smells of explosives because she had a friend who trained dogs for the Tulsa police. Sara had made sure both she and her wolf dog Skidi could recognize explosives by smell.

The subway car screeched again and pulled into Wall Street Station. The curious woman got up and left the car. Sara got up and followed her out.

Mystery Woman worried her. The Staten Island Ferry could wait.

# TWO

Once up to ground level, Mystery Woman checked the street signs —
Williams and Pine streets — and consulted a piece of paper in her
pocket. Then she moved north on Williams, her short legs moving
very fast to keep up with the crowd.

She walked hunched over, her head squished down on her shoulders and pointing halfway between the ground and forward. That in
itself wasn't unusual. Sara saw a number of New Yorkers walking
that way. But the woman also turned her head from side to side as
though she didn't want to miss anything.

Sara could see a lot of tourists also looking everywhere — not
wanting to miss anything. But those tourists didn't walk hunched
over. And they would often look up, up, up at the skyscrapers.
Mystery Woman never looked higher than the street signs.

Tourist or native? Sara was leaning towards native because the
woman walked direct and fast as though going to a meeting. But then
the woman looked at something clunky in her hand — her cell phone?

She was walking through a little triangular park with benches.
Suddenly she sat down on one and twisted her head around to look
carefully at people who had been walking behind her.

*She's checking for a tail!* thought Sara, who immediately glazed her eyes and continued straight as though deep in thought.

Sara saw a souvenir shop half a block ahead and gratefully stepped into it. She saw Yankees baseball caps. The cap was a good idea, but she just couldn't wear a Yankees cap. She'd lived in three cities, including Tulsa, and their baseball fans all hated the Yankees. Fortunately, the shop also carried other teams.

With a N.Y. Mets cap on her head, Sara crossed the street to a landscaped corner fronting a huge office building. She picked up a discarded newspaper then sat on a bench where she could see back down across the corner to the park bench where the woman still sat. Swarms of people passed by her and the woman. But she could see her every couple of seconds.

Sara didn't find the woman fun anymore. Puzzling out someone who looked out of place was very different from tailing someone who was checking for tails. Maybe this woman really was a terrorist.

For a nanosecond, she thought about contacting the police — but that was ridiculous. She could hear herself telling an officer, "It's serious because she smells wrong." She shook her head.

Three times Sara saw Mystery Woman check her device, then put it away. Finally — finally! — the woman got up and continued walking up Williams Street. Sara let her get a half block ahead, then followed.

They both walked six blocks until the street dead-ended at Pace University, where the Mystery Woman turned left. She crossed a noisy tangle of streets coming together from all angles, then turned right at another dead end.

*This is ridiculous,* thought Sara. *There are subway stops much closer to here than the one she used.*

When Sara also turned the corner, she saw the woman across the street. She was at a fence talking to a police officer who appeared to be guarding the gate to a park in front of New York's City Hall.

The visual was a little funny — the tiny woman's eyes were not much higher than the man's belt. He was a tall, hefty, red-faced

Irishman who must have weighed at least twice what she did —
maybe even three times her weight when you added in all the gun,
club, taser, radio phone, handcuffs, and other gear he was wearing.

Despite that, she was going face-to-face, or rather face-to-belt?,
with him. Her feet were planted and she was arguing.

*Time to do something rash,* Sara thought as she walked right up to
the gate.

She smiled. "What's the problem here?" she asked, in her
"helpful bystander" persona.

Mystery Woman startled and turned, stepping reflexively away
from Sara. Then her eyes narrowed. She opened her mouth to say
something but changed her mind and closed it.

The burly officer looked at Sara. "This area is closed to the
public," he told her.

Sara looked across at the steps leading up the building. There
were maybe 20 people milling around, including some press. Two
people were handing out campaign signs, with the name Fletcher on
them.

Mystery Woman finally spoke. She had a rich voice — too
powerful and deep for her tiny size. "Corbin Fletcher announces he
runs for U.S. senate. I am public so I am allowed to see."

"Lady," he said, with exaggerated patience, "like I told you, this is
just a photo op. They book a new one every hour here 'cause the pols
want their picture on the steps. Nobody gets in there without a pass
from the campaign. No pass, no entry. You want to see him; wait for
him to appear somewhere for real."

Sara wondered what the woman wanted with Fletcher. She
thought maybe she should be there when the woman did get close to
him. She turned to the police officer and asked, "Is there someplace
they all leave by? We could maybe see him then?"

"You too?" He frowned at Sara.

"Hey," Sara said, "maybe he'll become President someday. I
could tell my kids I met him."

"Yeah, sure," he said, dismissing her. "Closest you could get is up there on Centre Street. His limo will probably go out there."

"No thanks," Mystery Woman said. She turned abruptly and walked away, quickly.

Sara froze. So much for befriending the woman. Even worse — she couldn't follow her now that she had exposed herself.

"Is she OK?" asked the officer.

"I don't know," Sara said.

# THREE

An hour later, Sara was standing on the open bow of the Staten Island ferry boat — plowing across the water. It was the best tourist deal in the town, given that a round trip took about an hour and the price was free. The view was spectacular — and it included the Statue of Liberty. She got an extra thump of her heart looking at it.

Yes, Sara knew the founding fathers hadn't expected those freedoms to apply to women or blacks. But the goal of freedom — so eloquently expressed in the light held by Lady Liberty... Sara felt a little awestruck.

She moved outside of the cabin and leaned against the railing, watching people the size of mice crawling all over the island that housed the Statue. She watched seagulls swooping along in the wake of the boat. Sara inhaled deeply and relished all the water and life smells around her — all new to someone who had never before seen the ocean.

Sara walked around to the back of the boat and found an isolated spot. She pulled out her protected cell phone to call Mason Spencer in central Pennsylvania.

Mason was a half-Lupiti, 23-year-old computer genius who had just become her tech guru. Two years ago, Sara saved his life from a man who took lethal exception to Mason hacking him. Ever since, Mason had pestered her to join her missions. She said yes only three months ago, after he graduated from college.

Sara worried about him getting so involved in what her life had become. But she really needed his skills.

"I blew it," she said. "I thought I'd learn more by joining her, but I learned a lot less. After that, I couldn't keep following her."

Sara sent Mason the best of the not-very-good cell phone photos she'd taken of the woman's face.

"While you're running that," she added, "can you dig up anything you can find on this Corbin Fletcher? Especially anything about what he's scheduled to do or just likely to do today and tomorrow."

Three hours later, Sara was about to go out restaurant-browsing for dinner when Mason got back to her.

"Best I can do on Fletcher is a guess for tonight," he told her. "There's nothing scheduled — but he's been photographed at two previous art openings at the Bettleman Gallery in SoHo. Tonight they're opening an exhibit by a rising new artist named Rashid Guzman.

"Fletcher just had a breakup with a woman who has part owner-ship in the gallery — her name is Clary Livingston. Don't know if that makes him more — or less — likely to go there."

"Worth a try," Sara said. "Or...is it? Am I looking for trouble when there isn't any? I mean... I'm supposed to be on vacation!"

"Trust your instincts," said Mason. "They're the best I've seen. And... here's a big warning bell — I couldn't find this woman's face anywhere. The closest I got was a 90% match — and it's not her."

"Where'd you run her?"

"Everywhere — that's why I took so long calling you. I even tapped into arrivals in the U.S. over the past three weeks. Nothing."

"Is that unexpected?" asked Sara.

"If she were white — she'd have to be a space alien to not be found. But facial recognition isn't as reliable with black people's faces — companies have been sloppy. Cops have arrested the wrong man based on faulty matches. But even so — I should have found her.

"It's like she didn't exist until today."

Sara said. "I have this nagging feeling that Fletcher is in danger from her. Guess I'm going to a gallery opening."

# FOUR

The Bettleman Gallery was in the middle of the block on Grand Street. Its three large floor-to-ceiling windows were separated by white Corinthian columns — bright in reflected street lights which had just come on at six PM. A white fire-escape ladder was hoisted up and secured between the first and second floors. Sara wondered if she could jump that high in human form.

Why hadn't she tested herself yet?

Women in dazzling evening gowns and women in torn jeans with too much black eye makeup were both going in — alone or accompanied by men who blended into the scenery next to their ornate women.

Sara found a hole-in-the-wall coffee shop across the street. After making sure Mystery Woman wasn't inside, Sara found a table where she could see the gallery door and windows.

She had downloaded a picture of Clary Livingston, Corbin Fletcher's ex-girlfriend. She could see Clary standing right now — front and center — inside the gallery, lighted through the huge windows. She was an ice blond in her late 20s, looking like her family came over on the Mayflower. She was greeting people entering the gallery, standing next to a stunning black man, hair in cornrows, dressed all in designer black with a silver tie. Sara presumed he was the artist. The couple made a striking greeting committee.

The hours for the opening were 6-8 PM. Sara saw no sign of Mystery Woman or of Fletcher until a limo pulled up right before eight. She saw Fletcher step out of it — looking exactly like his campaign pictures. He was very Ivy League — about 10 years post-college. Handsome in a bland 6-foot, brown hair, elite-entitled way, but getting a little extra flesh pushing out his cheeks and hiding his cheekbones.

He was with an aide, Bertie Wilkinson, who had been in almost every photo Sara had found of Fletcher — like he was joined at the hip. Bertie could have been a cheap double for Fletcher — similar looks, except he was shorter, less attractive, and puffed out more — about 40 extra pounds more.

The two of them stopped on the sidewalk as the limo moved away. They looked in the windows at Clary and Rashid.

Fletcher froze for four or five seconds. Then he squared his shoulders and walked in the door with his aide/friend. Sara could almost hear him gritting his teeth.

Sara checked again for Mystery Woman, but she was nowhere. Sara got up and moved to the window of the coffee shop. She watched as Fletcher and pal walked up to Clary and Rashid. They didn't shake hands. Some words were said. Sara could only see the two men's backs, but she saw Clary and Rashid both being polite — and giving insincere smiles.

Then the two men veered off. Fletcher moved around the gallery, saying hello to other attendees, patting them on the back, and making like a politician in glad-hand mode. His aide trailed in his wake.

Sara came out of the coffee shop as the two men left. She saw them walk to the corner where the limo was waiting and get in. She thought about catching a cab and telling it to follow that limo, but something kept her where she was.

The gallery flashed its lights, and soon the attendees were leaving. Sara considered calling it a night. Mystery Woman seemed to have disappeared.

The gallery lights went out. Clary and Rashid came out with a skinny white man with a bush of slicked-back hair. He locked the door behind them and then hailed a cab and left. Clary and Rashid turned to stroll away, hand in hand. It was nice weather for a stroll — but given how high Clary's shoe heels were, Sara figured they were going someplace very near.

Sara followed them, hanging back half a block. The two looked happy with each other. New love. Sara remembered it from her failed marriage — all that glow that turned the world into your own little fairyland. She wished the couple better luck than she had found.

The couple walked a block and a half, passing mostly closed establishments and two homeless people sleeping in doorways. Halfway down the street, they turned towards one of the buildings and started fumbling in their clothes.

Sara kept walking, but slower. She looked around and saw nobody else walking on the block.

The building across the street had some interesting architectural frou-frou that Sara decided she liked. She was about to turn her head back to the couple — when she saw the building move. Or, rather, a figure moved forward from where he'd been lurking back against the building.

"He" because the figure turned out to be Corbin Fletcher.

Sara looked across the street and saw the couple disappearing into the building. She looked back at Fletcher. He just stood there, not moving — but somehow vibrating in energy. It came off him like he was a piece of uranium spewing out radiation.

*Not good!* Sara watched him stand there for a minute or so.

She had continued walking slowly and was now maybe a hundred feet from where the couple had gone in. Fletcher's jaw clamped tight and he started forward. He didn't even notice her as he crossed the street and grabbed the door the couple had used. He pulled it open and disappeared into the building.

Sara started moving faster.

A homeless lump of rags that had been huddled on the street just past the couple's building suddenly stood up and threw off his grimy blanket covering. Sara had seen several homeless people squatting against buildings in New York. She'd never seen one do that.

Surprise — the homeless man turned out to be the very short Mystery Woman, who moved quickly towards the door where Fletcher had gone.

Sara stopped walking, frozen in surprise.

Mystery Woman saw Sara and recognized her. She also froze — her face in shock and confusion. Then she shook her head emphatically at Sara and said, "No. Go away." And she hurried into the building after Fletcher.

*What the hell is this?* thought Sara. *Grand Central Station?*

Sara also started running. She went through the door about a minute later.

The entryway was narrow but clean. Mailboxes for the apartments lined one wall. Sara could see four apartment doors on this floor and an old-fashioned staircase going up. She started scanning the mailboxes, looking for Livingston or Guzman. She didn't know where to go. Then she heard a light popping sound. Seven pops.

The sound of a silenced pistol. Above.

# FIVE

Sara raced up a flight of stairs, turned a 180 on the landing, and sped up to the second floor. There were four doors here as well, but one of them was open. Sara hurried to it.

She stuck her head into an elegant sitting room with eggshell grass wallpaper and a dark purple couch big enough for a family. There were pale lime green silk curtains on the windows and a gorgeous Turkish rug on the floor.

All that tasteful design was overpowered by the sight of a massacre in the room. Six bodies were sprawled out in the room. Nobody was standing.

The stench was unbelievable. Sara liked the smell of blood — it was rich and full of subtle elements. She could do without — please! — the feces odors that always accompanied death.

There was an older black couple she had noticed earlier at the gallery. They were elegantly dressed and looked in their 50s. Each had a big red stain right where their hearts were. Both had been knocked back by the shots and were lying on the Turkish rug. The blood had poured out of them, surrounding each in a circle. But it had already stopped.

Clary and Rashid were lying next to each other, half on the polished oak floors and half up against a wall. Each had a heart shot like the older couple, but each of them had also been shot right in the face. Like someone wanted to obliterate them. Sara was sure it was them only by their clothes and their unique hair — her blond strands mixed with his cornrows — both now doused with red.

Fletcher was lying on his back close to the front window. He was sprawled out, looking dead, but she didn't see any blood on him. What she saw instead was a silenced pistol that had fallen. Next to his right hand.

Mystery Woman was lying closest to the door. She had been gut shot, but she was still alive. She had a long, thin knife lying by her right hand.

Sara walked over to where Fletcher lay. She leaned down and put a finger on his throat. His heart was beating steady. He was breathing.

Sara saw Mystery Woman sit up — face twisted in pain — and pick up her knife. She started crawling purposefully towards Sara, gasping with each movement.

Sara started towards her, but the woman veered away. She was actually crawling towards Fletcher — her eyes glued on him. She crawled like her life depended on it.

"You need a doctor," Sara said to her. She pulled out her cell phone, but the woman interrupted her.

"No!" she said, with a quick, penetrating look at Sara. Then she continued her desperate crawl forward. "I can't be found here. Dead anyway when I go home. Must finish the mission."

Mystery Woman reached Fletcher and took a deep breath. She scooted closer and sat up — eyes on her shoes. All casual-like. Then, quicker than a snake, she raised her hand with the knife — determined to plunge it as deep as she could into Fletcher's heart.

Sara had half expected this, but it still took all her speed to grab the woman's hand before the knife entered his body. The woman was strong. Very strong for her size and lack of weight. But Sara had wolf strength. It was no contest.

Tears sprang into the woman's eyes, but still she struggled. Until... Sara could see when the woman recognized her strength wasn't enough.

"You must let me," she pleaded with Sara — like it was the most important thing in the entire world. "He must die."

"Why?" Sara asked.

Frustration burned in the woman's eyes. She looked like she was struggling to find the words. She sighed in exasperation — as if it was impossible to explain.

"Why? You see what he did?"

She waved her hand at the four bodies on the floor. And at herself.

"Yes," Sara agreed.

"You see he killed Guzman's parents, too? Browns mean nothing to him."

"Browns?"

"People. You and me. Everyone except the Plutarchs."

Sara frowned at her. "He'll go to jail for this."

"No!" She shook her head. "He escapes this."

"No way," Sara said. "There's too much evidence. And... why is he just lying here? What's wrong with him?"

"I stunned him. Couldn't bring a gun through. Needed help. But he was quick. Shot me as he fell. I made mistake."

Suddenly her eyes went wide. "Oh, DeathEater! He comes!"

The woman tried to get her right hand into her pocket. Sara kept her grip on the woman's arm and stopped her. Whatever the woman wanted in her pocket should probably stay where it was.

The woman suddenly looked at Fletcher's gun and twisted in Sara's grip, trying to dive over his body to get at it. Sara stopped that as well.

Mystery Woman said in desperation. "OK. You take gun. Quick. Protect yourself."

"I'm not touching that gun. It proves Fletcher shot those people."

"You need it!" Mystery Woman pleaded. "Please!"

There were footsteps at the doorway.

"Too late," she said.

Fletcher's friend/aide — Bertie — stepped into the room. He looked first at Fletcher, lying there. Then he swept his eyes over all the blood and dead bodies. He looked at Sara and Mystery Woman, then he ran to Fletcher and pushed both women away. He knelt beside Fletcher to check his pulse — looking relieved to find one. Then he opened Fletcher's jacket — looking for wounds.

"What happened here?" he asked.

"Your friend killed four people and also shot her," said Sara, pointing at Mystery Woman. "That's what happened."

"Is Fletcher hurt?"

"She says he's just stunned. I guess he'll wake up soon."

Sara could see the thoughts racing around behind Bertie's eyes. She waited to see what he would do.

Bertie must have come to a conclusion. He nodded to himself. He got up and looked out the front bay window. Then he looked out in the hallway. He came back in and closed the door, and went back to Fletcher.

He picked up Fletcher's silenced gun, pointed it at Sara, and pulled the trigger again and again. Two bullets hit her in the shoulder, sending her crashing to the floor.

Sara screamed in pain and shock. "What the hell is wrong with you?"

Bertie kept the gun pointed at Sara and pulled the trigger again. And again. But the magazine must have been empty. Nothing fired.

He turned the gun to Mystery Woman and pulled the trigger again — still no effect — before giving up.

Sara put her feet under her, readying to put her fist into Bertie's face. Looking forward to it. But then her pain intensified. Beyond the shoulder pain came that too familiar agony. The pain of transforming. She felt the start of her mouth and nose reshaping themselves.

*Oh God no,* she said to herself. *Stop it. Stop it. Stop it right now!*

The aide wiped the gun carefully, removing all prints. Then he stepped carefully, avoiding all blood, over to Rasheed. He put the gun in Rasheed's right hand and shoved his index finger inside the trigger guard. He squeezed Rasheed's hand and finger to make good prints. Then he let the gun drop beside the man.

It took every bit of strength Sara possessed to fight the transformation. She absolutely could not become a wolf here. Cops would be here. She couldn't go anywhere in the city in wolf form. She would be caged. Discovered. Her teeth ground together. Sweat poured out her forehead and down her face.

*No! No! No!* Her brain screamed.

Mystery Woman jerked out of Sara's distracted grip and crawled to her knife. She picked it up and kept crawling — back towards Fletcher. She had no chance at all, but Sara was astonished at her determination. She got closer.

The aide noticed her. His foot moved as though to kick her. But he stopped. He was looking at all the blood that would get on his shoe. Instead, he bent down and lifted Fletcher, getting an arm around him, as if Fletcher was just drunk.

He glared at Mystery Woman and said to her, "You'll be dead in minutes."

He turned to Sara and said, "You'd better run. And keep your mouth shut if you want to live."

Then he walked out the door, mostly carrying Fletcher. He left the door open.

# SIX

Sara pulled herself together. She pushed the door closed with her elbow — no prints!

She moved to the front bay window, which overlooked the street she'd just been on. Nothing was there except the limo waiting for Bertie. She moved further into the apartment and found another window — which overlooked a small alley. She covered her hand with her jacket and tried the window. It opened and there was a fire escape there. She wouldn't be trapped in the apartment.

Sara ran back to the woman and said, "You need a doctor."

Mystery Woman shook her head. "I refuse. I die anyway. I was our only chance and I failed. Unless you help me?"

Sara stared into the woman's eyes. "Tell me just what the hell is going on here."

"You won't believe me."

"What have you got to lose?"

Mystery Woman gritted her teeth and held her breath as pain racked her. Then it must have eased slightly because she panted air back into her lungs.

"OK, sure," she said and rolled her eyes. "I come from year 2193."

Sara swallowed. *OK,* she thought, *I asked for it.*

"And?" Sara asked.

The woman looked at her, suspicious.

"I've learned to believe all sorts of impossible things," Sara said. She pointed at her shoulder. "This will be gone as soon as I change. The bullet wasn't silver."

The woman's eyes widened. "*Loups garous.* Good fighters for the Underground."

Sara's mouth gaped open. "You have more of us?"

The woman gritted her teeth and bent in pain. A moan escaped her lips.

Sara jumped up. She ran to the front and then the back windows. Still nobody. But that wouldn't last. And the woman wouldn't last. She ran back and knelt beside the woman.

"Why do you want to kill Fletcher?"

"What's your name?"

"Sara Flores."

"No name for me like that. Just Utility A-84-702. In my world, there are patriarchs and browns — everyone else. Different laws.

"Fletcher starts it. President in 14 years. He makes laws that make it hard for poor people to vote. My world — we have no vote.

"Fletcher stops passage of rule against perpetuities — so rich control all the money."

Her eyes shut, then she jerked them open. She took a deep breath and pulled out that clunky cell phone Sara had seen. But it wasn't a phone.

"I can't be found here," she said.

She reached out with her left hand and Sara took it.

"Many died to send me through machine. We not get another chance. Now *you* our only chance. Save the future. Fletcher cannot become President!"

Utility A-84-702 let go of Sara's hand then adjusted something on her device. And then she vanished.

Just poof. Right in front of Sara.

*Holy crap!*

# SEVEN

Sara was hyperventilating. She had to control her breath. She tried slowing it. Deep, slower breaths. Again. Again.

She looked down at herself. Two bullet holes showed in her jacket. Blood covered it and her shirt. Pain grabbed Sara again, now that the woman's story wasn't distracting her.

Jerking open the front closet, Sara found a light jacket that zipped closed. She grabbed it and a towel from the bathroom. She pushed the towel against her chest and struggled into the jacket.

*Ow! Ow! Ow!*

She stumbled to the back room and dragged open the window. *Slow breaths. Slow deep breaths.*

Wait! She ran back to the kitchen and looked in the fridge. "Thank god," she said as she grabbed a frozen steak, ripped it out of the plastic, and put it in the jacket pocket.

She ran back to the window and stepped out onto the fire escape, and closed the window behind her with her elbow — no prints! She stepped quickly but lightly — wincing at the metallic clang the stairs made with each step. She tried to look as casual as possible, strolling down the steps to the dirty, trash-can-filled alley. Strolling to the side street.

Sara heard nearby police sirens wailing. She walked — slowly, casually! — two blocks over to Broadway, holding her hand tight against her right chest, keeping the jacket and towel snug against her wounds. She flagged a cab and took it to the Hyatt hotel on West 57th Street, then walked back about 150 feet to the Salisbury Hotel, where she had her room.

She nodded at the front desk and walked — casually — to the elevators. Thankfully, she was alone in the elevator. She sighed in relief as she entered her room and double-locked it. She ran to the bathroom and lay down on the marble-looking floor — less blood to clean up later.

With a huge sigh, she let the transformation happen. For the first time since she became a werewolf, she didn't mind the pain of transforming. She just traded the gunshot pains for the transformation pain. Gladly.

The transformation, as always, popped out the bullets and healed her body of the damage.

Sara just lay there afterwards in wolf form — panting. Maybe she could sleep right here on the cold marble floor all night. The sink was there for water. What else did she need? And the toilet? Sara chuffed. That would be a sight — trying to use that in wolf form. It would make a great YouTube video. Maybe her wolf could become a video star.

Ok, she was getting silly now.

The lack of pain in her chest was the best feeling she'd ever had. She savored there being absolutely nothing wrong with her chest. She smiled a big wolf grin at the lack of pain in her snout and her spine after transforming. Nothing felt better than this.

Which is why she really, really, *really* didn't want to go through the pain all over again by transforming back.

Finally, she bit hard into the steak — partly still frozen — and chewed it down so she could transform back to human. Her mouth watered in delight, although her brain was less enthusiastic.

After the new pain — *remind me just why the hell I'm doing this?* — she ran a bath as deep as the tub would allow. She called room service and ordered a huge meal with cheesecake and roast chicken. Steak had lost its appeal for the moment. All to be delivered in an hour.

Then Sara climbed into the bubble-bath-filled soaker tub. She lay back, covering everything from her chin on down with the hot water. She felt her very taut muscles start to relax. They weren't really sore and abused — her transformation took care of that. But apparently her mind thought her muscles needed soothing — so the water did help. It brought a little peace of mind.

After the meal — eating slowly to savor it all — she texted Mason. She told him about the bodies and asked him to find out what the police were reporting on what they had discovered. She also told him not to contact her for the next eight hours unless the world ended.

Then she slept.

In the morning, Sara sat at a desk, eating off the room service tray. She had delicious eggs, sausage, and two blueberry muffins. She read the story in the provided *New York Times*, while watching it on CBS.

Up-and-coming artist Rasheed Guzman had apparently shot and killed both his parents and socialite Clary Livingston — before being gunned down by someone unknown. Sara read and watched until she'd learned all the reporters knew.

Mason called and said it would take a couple of days before internal police records would let him know if they were going to ignore what must have been confusing evidence at the scene.

Sara told him, "I know I didn't leave blood there, and I hope I didn't leave fingerprints. But I could have dropped some hairs. I know Mystery Woman left blood. No, not Mystery Woman — Utility A-84-702. She deserves her name.

"And how the hell could they think Rasheed did it? I'm pretty sure he didn't shoot himself twice to commit suicide."

Sara sighed. "I'm going home today. I have to think. Fletcher's comments to the press made me want to throw up."

"This was a terrible tragedy," Corbin Fletcher said on the eight AM news. "Clary was a wonderful woman who didn't deserve to die. There is a lawlessness across our country that just sickens me. Something must be done about it." He looked appalled.

Standing right behind him was his aide, Bertie Wilkinson. The man who had shot Sara.

# EIGHT

Sara was happy to be back in her high-tech, protected home which looked like a modest farmhouse with a wrap-around porch. It was on a bank of the Arkansas River near Tulsa.

She sat for hours on the patio in her plastic fake Adirondack chair and watched the muddy river float by. She ruffled her wolf-dog Skidi's fur — and threw the ball for her. She cooked. She even got on a cleaning jag. One night Sara took the two of them to the desert outside of Santa Fe — where they could run the night away as wolves.

Sara told Mason everything that had happened.

"So you and I will be 'browns' in the future?" Mason asked. "Because you're half Mexican and I'm half Lupiti?"

"I had so little time to talk to her," Sara said. "But it sounded like everyone will be 'browns' except the billionaires. They become the Plutarchs and control everything."

"And how is that different from today?"

"In scope. Think about her name — Utility A-84-702. It sounds like the browns are named only for the job they do. Think what would have to be different for that to happen. Maybe brown babies are allowed or grown only for specific jobs. Because the Plutarchs need masses of people to do all the work they don't want to dirty their hands with."

Mason told Sara the New York police were looking for an unidentified shooter — but not very hard. They accepted Rasheed as the killer of his parents and Clary. They absolutely were not looking at Fletcher.

Sara spent the next two days locked inside her head. She was wrestling with her thoughts — and she was losing.

One day in total frustration, she called Bill Hanalho, the new chief of the Lupiti priests. "I could use a spiritual advisor," she told him.

Which was actually funny. When they last met, she'd had a very different idea of how to "use" him. The man was a hunk. He looked thirty-something, tall, black hair almost to his waist, wonderful body — strong but not muscle-bound. Great hands. And a good heart.

Six months ago, Sara had gone to his grandfather — the head Lupiti priest at the time — to try to talk with Joe White Wolf's spirit — the Lupiti shaman who had turned her.

Pretty much everything went very wrong that night — including her transforming against her will. Bill's grandfather ended up dead — not her fault, thankfully. Bill inherited the job and he knew her secret. Because he knew werewolves existed, she thought he might be open to the possibility of time travel.

And it was a great excuse to see him again(!)

She and Bill met out by Lupiti Lake, which wasn't crowded at the moment. Just two families were sitting on park benches and a couple was paddling a canoe. She walked with him out onto the pier and they sat with their legs hanging over the side — almost to the water.

They really shouldn't be seen together. In Lupiti culture — a priest and a shaman were antagonists. Bill was now the head priest. Since the man who transformed Sara was a shaman, that made her sort of a shaman. They were like the Hatfields and McCoys of Lupiti society.

Sara grimaced as she remembered Mason's opinion — that she

enjoyed fantasizing about Bill because she knew nothing could ever come of it. It wasn't *her* fault she couldn't have the man she most wanted.

Was it?

Sara told him everything, and Bill didn't interrupt. When she finished, he asked if she believed the woman was from the future.

"You mean, despite the fact that time travel is impossible?" She grinned.

"Yeah, despite that."

"There are quite a few small reasons to believe her. But mainly there's that 'vanishing into thin air' thing."

Bill said, "So why are you trying not to believe her?"

Sara rubbed her hands over her eyes. "Because if I believe her, I have to decide whether to complete her mission."

"It's the Hitler question. Isn't it?"

"Exactly," said Sara, relieved at his understanding. "It's the old, 'If you could go back in time and kill Hitler when he was young, would you?' Except that's supposed to be a fun mind-game instead of a serious question."

Bill just looked at her.

"Because," Sara continued, "if I do this, I'll be killing in cold blood. Worse even — I'd be killing someone for what he hasn't done yet."

Bill reached out and took her hand. "How do you feel about killing?"

"In self-defense, I'd kill anyone and sleep like a baby," said Sara. "That's easy. It's a little more complicated when I kill someone on one of my missions. Then it's someone who has killed others and intends to kill the person I'm trying to help. Or to kill me, when I try to stop them. So it's really just self-defense — expanded to include the defense of others."

Bill smiled at her.

"Yes, I know," she said. "I've thought this out in excruciating detail. I haven't thought of much else the past week."

"Will it hurt you to kill him?"

"I don't think I'll really know unless I do it. What bothers me the most is — will I hurt the world if I don't kill him?"

Bill smiled and shook his head. "You don't have a problem with boredom in your life, do you?"

Sara grinned. "Not recently, no."

Bill said, "You know that saying — 'All that's necessary for the triumph of evil is for good men to do nothing'?"

"Exactly. How can I do nothing?"

"But... I doubt very much the point of that quote was to justify killing."

"I know. You're right."

They sat there, both thinking. Sara looked up through the brush at the sky overhead. She saw a hawk circling. It was a beautiful day. It felt good sitting there. By Bill. She really liked him.

Sara turned and looked at him. She wondered what all the priests did in their ceremonies. "Say, *you* don't turn into anything, do you? A hawk? A chipmunk?"

Bill grinned. "Sorry, priest business stays only with priests."

"It's not fair! You know about me."

Bill patted her on the shoulder. "I'm pretty sure nobody told you life was fair. And... if they did, you wouldn't have believed them."

"No, it's not fair." She shook her head.

"And..." she continued, "if Utility A-84-702 is right, it will get a lot more unfair. I looked up what she said — that part about a 'rule against perpetuities.' We have laws that let the rich avoid paying any taxes on wealth growth — as long as they don't sell. It's causing income disparity to mushroom between the top 1% and the rest of Americans. What she described could happen."

Bill stood up. "Let's go back. "You already know what you intend to do."

Sara stood up too.

Bill frowned at her. "Just be careful, Sara. New York City is not here. There's no easy way to hide a body."

Sara laughed.

"I'm serious. If you go, you can't afford to hesitate. People here need you. You have to come back."

Sara looked at him. "Well, it's nice to know you care."

Bill took off walking to his truck. Over his shoulder, he said, "I don't."

Sara followed him to his truck and watched him get in. Then she leaned in his driver-side window.

"Bullshit you don't care," she said. Then she softly patted his door and walked back to her F150.

# NINE

Mason searched online and found the luxury condo Fletcher owned in the Staten Island section of New York. It was worth about two million and paid for in cash.

"He's a self-made man," Mason told her, "once daddy kicked in almost three million."

Unfortunately, the condo was no place to confront him. It was on the waterfront, with no connection to local streets. You couldn't walk anywhere from there — only drive. That meant a secure entrance and exit. His buddy Bertie Wilkinson lived there with him, and one or both of them frequently brought home a woman. So even if Sara could get in — it would be problematic.

During the day, as Fletcher moved from meeting to meeting to photo opportunity, he was surrounded by flunkies. More flunkies than just Bertie.

Mason dug up two SoHo nightclubs Fletcher frequented most often. One was the Rumpus Room, on Eldridge. The other was The Blond, on Howard St.

Two weeks later, Sara was back in Manhattan.

She checked out the location of both of Fletcher's favorite clubs.

The Rumpus Room had two different "parks" within a block. They were called parks, but they were no more than one-block concrete-surfaced open spaces with a few benches and tree pots. They were very, very exposed — there were over a thousand apartments looking right down at them. Anyone in those "parks" might as well be performing on stage!

The Blond looked better. Howard Street was narrow — with bumper-to-bumper cars parked on one side of it. A stopped truck there would block any through traffic. Blick Art Materials — directly across from it — would be closed late at night. And there was scaf-folding over both sides of the street. That included built-out plywood overhangs between the street level and the next floor up — to catch any construction debris.

The buildings on Howard Street were only four or five stories tall — not like the high rises over on Eldridge. And these four or five stories couldn't see anything on the sidewalks below due to the plywood overhangs.

Also good, there was a five-story parking garage just catty-corner to the club. Just in case things got dicey.

The big problem was finding when Fletcher would go to that club. In the meantime, Sara moved to the Solita SoHo hotel — roughly two blocks from The Blond — and on the opposite side of the parking garage.

She liked the street the Solita was on. It looked like the West Side Story movie, with lots of buildings each with its own fire escape. Here each building and fire escape were painted a different bright primary color — first green, then red, then yellow. She also liked the lobby with its fancy wood-slat check-in desk. There was a huge picture behind it of a Geisha-white woman's face with bright red lips. She especially liked that the room rate was half the daily price of the exclusive, upscale hotel that was attached to The Blond.

Mason solved part of their problem. He found the limo company Fletcher used when he went out partying. It was Four Stars Limo, based in a luxury apartment building in lower Manhattan. They had a street-level studio apartment for an office, plus three parking spaces in the building — enough for three non-stretch limos.

Sara slipped into their garage one night and attached GPS trackers to all three of the limos.

She also did a careful walk-through of the parking garage between her hotel and The Blond. She hid a change of clothes behind a filthy column in the garage. She hid beef jerky — sealed inside three freezer bags, one bag inside the other — just in case she had to transform back to human. Quickly.

Then Sara pulled out a big pink dog collar that fit her in wolf form and hid it behind a third column. The collar was in case every-thing went totally, completely to hell. Her hotel took dogs. It was at least theoretically possible she could stroll into the hotel as a pretend dog staying there — and make it up to her room. She hoped she didn't have to try it.

Then it was just a wait.

In the mornings, Sara did the tourist bit. She liked the oddball stuff you would never find elsewhere. Like the all-pink Museum of Ice Cream — with delicious samples for the tasting. And the Museum of Feelings — which changed colors on its outside walls based on the current "mood" of the city itself. Although... she was curious as to who determined what the city's mood was each day.

She was less sure about the city's Museum of Jello and the Museum of Sex. The latter featured a life-sized statue of three elk, all humping, one on top of the other.

Afternoons she took a long nap, followed by a great dinner. She tried only unusual foods she'd never heard of before — food she wouldn't find in Tulsa. She tried kangaroo burgers, curried lamb brain, chorizo caramel swirl ice cream (yum!), and a lox rice bowl.

She refused to try grasshopper tacos — one had to draw a line *somewhere.*

Evenings she spent pacing the room — waiting to hear from Mason.

One night passed. Another. She tried to check out the Tenement

Museum — but it made her nauseous and she had to run out. It showed the terrible living conditions of immigrants back in the 1800s and early 1900s. It looked too much like what Sara suspected Utility A-84-702's world might look like for everyone not rich.

The next ten times Sara thought about just checking out of her hotel and going home, her mental images of what she saw at that museum steeled her resolve.

It was Thursday at 10PM when Mason finally called. Fletcher had rented a limo.

Sara got ready. She dressed in simple black with thin surgical flesh-colored gloves. It complimented her curly red-haired wig and heavy makeup. She carried a stiletto (least likely to get hung up on a bone on its way to the heart) and a small squeeze bottle loaded with botox powder.

Sara wanted to scream when Mason's next call told her the limo was outside the Rumpus Room. Sara paced. She sat. She watched TV without knowing what she was watching.

Mason called again two hours later. The limo was moving south-west in the direction of The Blond. Sara took the elevator down. She went outside and walked the two blocks to the club. As she walked up towards it, she saw three thirty-something richly dressed men and two women leaving it. Sara looked down at her watch. As though she was expecting someone. Which, of course, she was.

Her phone vibrated. She looked and saw a text from Mason. The limo was one block away.

"If it's not right, you can wait and try another night," Sara reminded herself. But she really, really didn't want to wait.

The limo pulled up in front of the club.

*Will the driver get out?* Sara wondered. But he didn't. Bertie got out, then Fletcher. And no women. Yet. And nobody else on the sidewalk.

Sara turned towards them. "Corbin?" she asked, looking at Fletcher. She gave her biggest smile and walked towards them.

"It's been ages!" she said. "How have you been?"

Sara noticed the limo move away to wherever limos disappear in New York until you call them back.

Corbin Fletcher stood there, racking his brain as to who she might be of the thousands of women he'd met socially. Eyeing her to see if he wanted more from her.

She was almost to him, left hand in her pocket and right hand rising up as though to shake, the stiletto in it hidden from view.

Suddenly, however, Bertie saw past the wig and makeup and recognized her.

"No!" he yelled as he grabbed and jerked Corbin's hand.

It moved Corbin slightly so while the stiletto went into his chest, Sara wasn't sure it hit the heart. She continued her forward motion and brought the two of them down onto the sidewalk, slamming her knee into the concrete and bouncing his head. She twisted her right hand, still holding the blade, around inside of him. At the same time, she brought out her left hand with the tiny squeeze bottle in it. Fletcher's mouth was open, and she shoved the plastic bulb inside his jaws and squeezed the powder out.

Corbin pushed her off and struggled to rise. Sara stood. "For your sins," she said and kicked him in the head. He slammed back and was still.

Sara withdrew an envelope from her jacket and placed it inside Corbin's jacket.

Bertie had stepped back, eyes wide. His mouth was open as if he wanted to call out but wasn't sure if he should. He was also fumbling in back of his waistband, trying to get to a gun he must have started carrying there.

Sara put her right arm around him, squeezing tight. The hold pinned his left arm against her, and his right arm was held tight by her hand. If someone saw them, she hoped it looked like a friendly hug. Bertie couldn't move either arm to get to his gun.

"Bertie, Bertie," she said. "You and I have so much to talk about." She started walking with him towards the corner, dragging him along easily with her enhanced strength.

Bertie struggled, surprised he couldn't get out of her one-armed hold. He twisted his head to look back at Fletcher as she dragged him further away.

"Oh, don't worry about him," she said. "He'll be fine. A little bruised up. You'll see him tomorrow."

Bertie struggled even harder, but his arms were trapped, and she was controlling him. His feet moved involuntarily as if his body was afraid he'd otherwise fall, but her arm really carried him. Just high enough to make his feet bumble along instead of being obviously dragged.

Bertie opened his mouth again, this time determined to call out. Sara's left hand came out and she moved it in front of Bertie's eyes. Only it wasn't a hand. She had transformed just her left hand into a paw with pads and fur and four very long claws.

"Focus, Bertie," she said, with a friendly smile on her face. "Focus on my hand. Or should I say, my paw? See these very, very sharp claws? One swipe and your jugular vein is completely gone. You'd bleed to death in a couple of minutes. Nothing anyone could do."

At the street corner, a couple was crossing — maybe 50 feet from them. Taxis and a few cars drove by.

"Be smart, Bertie. You do anything to attract their attention and you're dead in less than two minutes. If you keep quiet, we're just going over there because I have a story I want to tell you.

"Don't you want to know who I am?" She waved her paw in front of his eyes. "...and why I need you and Fletcher out of commission for a week?"

Bertie's eyes crossed, staring at the paw in front of his eyes. "How are you doing that?" he asked.

She walked him into the parking garage and up to the second floor, where her backpack and food were stashed. It was away from the elevators and stairs, behind two parked cars.

"Have a seat, Bertie."

He looked down, horrified.

"I know, I know," she said. "But you're rich — you can afford another suit if this one gets dirty." Sara pushed him down on the ground. Then she sat crosslegged, about three feet in front of him.

"It's a story about a woman," she said. "That's how I got involved in this. The woman was following Fletcher, and I was following her." Sara wasn't sure why she wanted to tell him about the woman. But she went with her instinct.

"...and," Sara concluded, "the woman said Fletcher would ruin the future by doing those two things when he became President."

Bertie had looked more and more dismissive as she told it, but at the end, he looked appalled.

"You're crazy!" he said. "You just attacked a man because you think someone from the future said you should?"

"Well... she painted a really awful picture. What else could I do?"

Bertie started to rise. Sara motioned with her hands for him to stay down. "No, no. That's not the real reason. Let me finish."

Bertie sat back down.

"I did it because he shot five people in that room. Killed four of them. And even then, I waited until it was clear he was going to get away with it.

"Oh and I told you one little lie. Fletcher is dead. I put enough botox in his lungs to kill half this town."

# TEN

Bertie jerked to his feet, furious. Sara rose as well. She was standing about three feet in front of him.

"Think twice before you draw that gun of yours," she said. "You already shot me once and it didn't take. Don't piss me off by doing it again."

"You stupid bitch! Fletcher is important. Powerful. He *could* become President. You threw away a chance to..."

"Fletcher was a racist, elitist asshole who thought the laws don't apply to him. I did the world a favor."

"But... you could have..."

"Sucked up to him like you did? Enabled him?"

Bertie's face was red. His right arm went under his coat.

"Last warning. Shoot me, and you're dead."

"No," he said. "You're dead."

Bertie pulled his gun to kill her, but Sara had expected it. Maybe wanted it even.

She grabbed the barrel of the pistol with her right hand and jerked it up fast and hard, ripping his forefinger off the trigger. At the same, time her left hand closed around his throat. She pushed him back and up against a concrete wall and held him there as her right hand stuffed the gun in her jacket pocket. His feet were dangling off the ground.

"Big mistake, Bertie. You forgot about the most important question you asked me. Remember?"

Bertie struggled. He hit her in the head with his right fist, but it barely hurt. Because of the wall behind him, his punch could barely travel a foot before landing. A martial artist could have managed some strength in that short a punch, but it was obvious Bertie wasn't one.

Sara cocked her eyebrow at him.

"Focus, Bertie. Remember what you asked me on the way here? No? Need a hint?"

She put her right hand in front of his face and twisted it around. She kept it human, but surely he hadn't already forgotten the paw?

Sara shook her head.

"You deserve to die, just like your pal, Bertie. You walked into a room, saw what Fletcher had done, and shot the witness — me. Then you covered it all up for him.

"I must be some kind of soft bleeding-heart idiot because I gave you another chance. Which you failed."

Sara increased the pressure of her left hand on his throat — to make sure he couldn't cry out. Then she looked around just to be sure. And scented the air. They were alone here on this floor of the garage.

Sara started the transformation of her face only. Her mouth and her nose started moving forward in her face — in unison. Joining into a snout. Bertie's eyes grew wide as her snout moved closer and closer to him. Once it was fully formed, Sara opened her jaws. She displayed all 42 of her gleaming white — long! — teeth.

Bertie panicked. He fought to get away with everything he had — twisting and punching. He even landed a truly pathetic kick. He tried to scream, but all that got past his constricted throat were whimpers and whines. When he could see it did no good, he stopped strug-gling and closed his eyes.

Sara let go of him. He stumbled, then righted himself. His eyes popped open. His mouth opened — he was going to scream at the top of his lungs.

Sara leaned forward, turned her head sideways, and bit Bertie's head right off his neck. Blood gushed out everywhere, spraying her clothes, the column, the wall and the filthy concrete floor.

# ELEVEN

Sara pushed the headless body away from her. She grabbed her bag from behind the column while she transformed her face back to human. She took off her bloody clothes and wiped off her shoes. She quickly redressed with her bag clothes and repacked the bloody ones, also wiping the gloves.

She removed Bertie's gun from her pocket and broke it into pieces, then started moving away at a New-York-normal quick pace. Her gloves prevented fingerprint worries, so she dropped the bullets in a trash bin on the ground floor as she exited the parking garage.

Sara found two rain gutters in the two blocks leading to her hotel. She put half the gun pieces down one drain and the other half down the other. Then she peeled off and pocketed the gloves.

As she passed a parked car, Sara looked at her face in its side mirror. She patted her hair and twisted her mouth as though she was primping. What she was really looking for was blood. She wiped away the one splotch she saw on her cheek. She also saw some red droplets in her hair, so she pinched them and pulled them down over the strands — turning them into red highlights.

Sara tilted her head at the effect. They looked kind of good — she might have her hairdresser give her some red streaks in the future.

At three AM, even most New Yorkers were in bed. She saw one couple as she entered her hotel. They were so preoccupied with each other they didn't even see her. She nodded at the desk man and got into the elevator alone.

She texted Mason it was done, then took a long hot shower. When done, she filled the tub with cold water and dumped her blood-soaked clothes from the bag into it to rinse out the blood. In the morning, she'd dump the dried, no-visible-blood clothes at a shelter.

The hotel only offered sandwiches at this hour so she got a wonderful roast beef with avocado and Swiss cheese from room service.

Finally, she called Mason. Mason kept hacker hours, so three AM was the middle of his workday.

"You left the envelope on Fletcher?" he asked.

"Yes," she said. "Like we agreed. It was addressed to the police and confessed to killing Clary, Rasheed and his parents. It also said he'd tried to make amends for it financially."

"He had $1.4 million in U.S. banks," said Mason. Today, about an hour before his death, he generously donated $1 million of it split between the NAACP and Feeding America. I left him $400,000. I figured nobody would believe he'd give away everything."

"Good! Something positive. Ah... I guess you couldn't find any hidden accounts?" Sara covered her mouth to prevent him from hearing even the hint of a laugh in her voice.

There was a long silence. "This isn't going to work if you insult me, Sara."

Sara's grin grew bigger. She tried to sound innocent. "You mean you *did* find something?"

"You're laughing, aren't you?"

"You're so easy to tease! Tell me what you found?"

"Fletcher had almost $2 million in a hidden account on the island of Nevis. Now we each have half of it."

"Wait, I thought you said the Caribbean was no longer a tax haven."

"Nevis is a holdout. Corporations formed there are among the most secret of anywhere."

"But not good enough to stop you. I may tease you, but I really am impressed."

"As you should be," Mason said, hiding how much he wanted to hear those words.

"So, what are you going to do with your half," she asked?

"I'm keeping about $75,000 of it. I need better equipment and better security here. But I'm thinking the other $920,000 would be a great start to an education nonprofit for Native Americans. It could provide financial help to stay in high school, as well as scholarships for college."

"That's a great idea, Mason!"

"What about your half?" he asked.

"I don't need any more myself," Sara told him. "But I want to start a fund. I'm worried about the future for wolves, given global warming. More and more people are going to buy land further north. It's already happening in Montana. I'm afraid wolves in the wild are going to disappear.

"I'm going to start looking for a very big plot of land in Alaska to buy. I think I'll need one very big stash to do it. I'm going to call it a wildlife sanctuary — and it will be. But it will be primarily to protect lands where wolves can continue to roam."

Sara was ready to hang up when she heard him ask, "Do you think this did it? Changed the future to better?"

# TWELVE

"I wish I knew," she said. "I've been reading time travel books. Fiction, of course. But still interesting. Some of them imply that trends are almost impossible to erase. If you change something, the future finds another way to end up in almost the same spot it would if nothing had been done."

"So if someone really did go back and kill baby Hitler, all that fascism would happen anyway, and someone else would lead it?"

"That's one theory."

"That would suck. I hope it's wrong."

"Me too," said Sara. "But think about the good you're about to do. Utility A-84-702 did what she could do. We did all that we could do."

"Well..." said Mason, "maybe not entirely. There's more *you* could do."

"Me? Like what?"

"Seems to me you need to find a mate and start raising a bunch of werewolf pups."

"*Excuse me??*"

Mason was laughing so hard he couldn't talk. Sara wanted to take the phone and smash it on his head.

Mason tried to talk, pulling himself together. "Sorry, just the image of you and pups."

"I'm hanging up."

"No, no, don't. I'm sorry. I'm sorry. But I'm also serious. Utility A-84-702 said the *loups garous* were good fighters for the Underground. So just in case time bends back around to that future — somebody needs to make sure there are werewolves there to help them. Seems to me you're the only one who can do that."

"But..."

"And that sanctuary sounds like the perfect place to raise them."

Mason hung up.

Sara sat there, staring at her phone. And staring at it. Finally, she closed her eyes and laid the phone down.

"Oh hell," she said. "He may be right."

END

Author of *Betrayal in Oklahoma* and *Curiosity Kills*

# SUE DENVER

"It's like Jack Reacher and Jane Yellowrock parented a kid who can use either a gun or fangs to take out bad guys." -*MJ Silversmith, Discovery*

# The Stench of Fear

A WolfLady™ Paranormal Mystery Novella

# ONE

Sara Flores believed you should stay away from cops when you have a really big secret. Cops are suspicious by training — by their nature as well — and they are very good at knowing when you're hiding something.

In the past year, since Sara became a werewolf, she'd made it her mission to rescue people trapped or being abused by powerful assholes. To complete her missions, she usually had to make those abusers become *dead* assholes.

Twice now she'd run into cops in the vicinity of a dead body she'd caused. Twice she'd managed to talk her way out of it.

Continuing on like this would be pretty stupid.

Sara decided, instead, to get a private investigator license. It would explain to suspicious cops why she might be in dark alleys any normal woman would go far out of her way to avoid.

How was she to know that decision — to get her license — would cause so many deaths?

To get that license, Sara found herself early one evening in a crappy classroom at People's Tech of Tulsa. The state of Oklahoma requires just 55 hours of training and passing a test — and voila! — you're a licensed P.I.

This classroom had small, high prison-like windows that gave off no light because the sun was already down on a cold February evening. And the smell... some mixture of chalk, carbon and body sweat — made Sara feel like she was back in 10th grade. It wasn't a fond memory.

She was sitting in one of those old high school desk/chair combos that you have to swivel into in order to sit down. They are so uncomfortable that you spend the entire class squirming around and watching the clock until you can free yourself.

Sara fidgeted some more and looked around at her "classmates." Eight of the 16 torture chairs were filled and she had a good view of them, as she was sitting in the back row.

There was a married couple, the Lauriers, upfront and center. Both were in their late 20's. Both were bright-eyed and scrubbed clean like new pennies.

There were three had-to-be cops sitting to Sara's right. Each had those hyper-observant cop eyes that could describe everything and everybody in a place within just a few minutes. Sara had expected to see some cops who were approaching retirement age in the class. Ones who were considering hanging out a private investigator shingle after leaving the force.

Two of them fit that bill. One was a big, white slab of beef about 50-something with a shaved head. The other was a black woman who could have been anywhere from 40-60 — it was hard to tell.

The third probable-cop was different. He looked in his 30s — which made Sara wonder just why he was here. He was white with light brown buzz-cut hair. Average height. Average build. He had an above-average smile, however, under a trim mustache. The smile showed because he was joking with the other two cops.

The teacher for this class finally walked into the room. Mr. Andersen — "Call me Greg" — was a good-looking older man with neatly trimmed gray hair. Although... there was something smarmy about him.

By the end of the three hour class, Sara — and the cops — hadn't written a single note. There wasn't much point in writing down things like, "You should show respect to the interviewee — even if you suspect them of lying."

*Well, duh!* thought Sara. *Thank god this part of the training is only 35 hours.*

Two evenings later, she was back with her classmates facing another three hours of Andersen. But this class promised to be more interesting — it was supposed to include reading body language.

Andersen handed out a sheet titled, "Body language that could indicate untruthful answers." Then, as if they were incapable of reading it for themselves, he read through each item.

"Lip biting — shows anxiety.

"Crossed arms — can be defensive or closed off.

"Eyes open very wide — surprise.

"Eyes narrowed — anger.

"Thumb up — agreement.

"Thumb down — disagreement."

Sara put her hand over her eyes — so she could roll them to express her opinion of these "incredible" insights. She couldn't believe she was paying actual money for this.

Andersen finished his reading and asked if there were any questions. Sara slammed her teeth closed — to prevent any of the sarcastic remarks on the tip of her tongue from flying out.

The woman cop — Velena Davis was her name — raised her hand. She said, "I heard if you're questioning someone and they look up and to their left — they're accessing their memory. But if they look up and to the right — they're creating a lie."

Andersen smiled. "You'll see that in a lot in articles, but it's not true. It was tested recently with a large group of volunteers. Half were instructed to lie about where their cell phone was and the other half were told to tell the truth. Then they were interviewed in front of a camera. There was no difference between the truthful group and the liars as to whether they looked up. Or in what direction."

*OK,* thought Sara. *I got one good tidbit from this class.* Because she had heard the same thing as the cop.

"Now, let's break up the class with a little role-playing," said Andersen. He handed out another sheet of paper.

This paper said, "You've been hired to discover who is stealing equipment from a company. There are three employees who have enough access to be able to pull it off."

Andersen said, "We'll switch off being the interviewer or the subject. If you're playing the subject, you decide if you are innocent or guilty." He gave the class a little time to consider.

Then he asked Sara to come up and run through it with him to show the class. Andersen role-played interviewer first. After some bland questions, he surprised her with, "Do you use illegal drugs?"

Sara raised her eyebrows at this, but answered truthfully, "No."

Andersen watched her, curiously intent. Sara got the idea her answer disappointed him.

Then they switched places. Sara asked Andersen questions, easy to start with. Then she tried to surprise him. Payback. She asked, "Have you committed a recent felony?"

Andersen gave her a very calm "No," with no lying indicators from his body language. In fact, she could see he was expecting some surprise question, although not that one.

But Sara knew immediately that Andersen was lying.

He controlled all his body language — but he couldn't control his sweat glands. When she asked the question, he gave off a sudden, sharp, acrid smell. It was so faint she knew nobody else in the class could smell it. But to a wolf nose — even one currently in human form — it was unmistakable. And it came instantly when she asked the question.

She wondered what kind of recent felony Andersen was committing.

Suddenly she pulled her attention back. Andersen was looking at her with a questioning look.

*Oh, hell!* she thought. *He knows I caught something.*

Andersen stood up, smiled, and waved her back to her desk.

"Thank you, Miz Flores. Now turn your desk to a neighbor, and each of you complete the exercise."

The rest of the class was at least entertaining. Sara took turns doing the exercise with the young cop — Mike Walsh was his name. His smile was even better when he turned it on her.

Mike had a friendly, almost puppy-dog personality, but he was also a champion liar. He gave nothing whatsoever away when he lied — except for the smell only she could detect. He knew he was good at it, so it annoyed him that she found him out each time.

Sara had fun with the assignment. But three times, when she wasn't looking forward, she could feel Andersen's eyes on her. Intently.

What kind of felony could he be committing that would make him that anxious?

# TWO

After class, Velena Davis caught up with her on the way to the parking lot.

"Want to get a cup of coffee?" she asked. "Joe's Joe is about a block away, and it's not terrible."

Sara debated. She liked this woman for some reason. But... keeping a low profile with cops doesn't mean hanging out with them, does it?

Sara must have thought about it too long, because Velena's eyes shuttered. "No problem," she said. "It's getting late."

"No," Sara said, "I'd like to. I was just running over what I need for an appointment tomorrow morning. But I'll be OK. Let's do it."

Joe's Joe was an interesting mix of design. It had black walls with rich walnut trim, counters, and tables. Trendy, but a touch of country. The snacks bar had regular sandwiches with a few more Southern Cal things like avocado and sprouts. The black coffee mugs were generous and the plain coffee was apparently delicious as it made Velena smile when she sipped it. They even had green tea for Sara.

Velena Davis turned out to be an interesting woman. She was about Sara's 5'7" — so they stood eye to eye. Velena was a little chunkier — but Sara suspected a large part of that was muscle. Otherwise, she probably wouldn't have advanced to police detective.

They commiserated with each other about paying actual money for the class. They also agreed that Andersen was a slime ball, who undressed women with his eyes.

"But... just young women," said Velena. "Or whites. He didn't give me his fish-belly eye, thank god."

Both women shuddered. Then laughed. Velena's smile lit up her face.

She told Sara she'd joined the Tulsa PD just over 19 years ago, back when being both black and a woman were a much bigger liability than today.

"How did you have the guts?" Sara asked. "I'd be worried about it today — I can't imagine 20 years ago."

"Two reasons," Velena said. "One was we needed the money, and it was better than most other jobs I could get. And second — I wanted to make a difference. I wanted to protect people. I know it sounds naive, but..."

"It sounds pretty good to me," Sara said.

Sara told Velena about her hermit life in Colorado — getting over a bad divorce. And how she came here because she didn't want to hide out anymore.

They chit-chatted about restaurants and good 'ole boys. Then Velena sat back, sipping her coffee. Her eyes were tight on Sara's.

"So," she said. "Will you tell me what you saw in Greg Andersen? When you asked if he'd committed a recent felony?"

Sara leaned back. "What do you mean?"

"I just read some tension there. First in you and then in him."

Sara thought a long time — trying to figure out if it could come back and bite her. Maybe not — if she pretended there was some doubt.

"OK," she said. "I'm just 99% sure he was lying — that he really *has* committed a recent felony. It just surprised me."

"What do you base it on?"

"I'm kind of a human lie detector." Sara smiled ruefully while lying shamelessly. "I was pretty good as a kid and got really good during my marriage. I am occasionally wrong — but it's very rare."

Velena tilted her head and raised an eyebrow.

Sara held up her hand. "Don't smirk! I'll bet you're pretty good at it yourself. After all the lies you hear in your job!"

"Of course. But I'm not 99%."

Sara asked herself if she wanted to push this and decided the answer was yes. Velena could bring resources Sara didn't have. If she got curious.

"Well..." Sara said. "I could give you a demonstration, but I'd have to ask a personally embarrassing or upsetting question. You'd have to answer yes or no, but I'd end up knowing if you lied. I did it once before, and the person never talked to me again. It's very intrusive."

"Show me — I can handle it."

Sara shook her head. "I'm not joking — you'll hate me. It has to be a very rude question — like I did asking about a felony to Andersen. Because I think part of what I pick up is smell — sweat glands. I have a very sensitive nose."

"I can handle it."

Sara thought harder. "I'm a little afraid to try it with a police detective. I suspect one reason people join the police is a desire to be in control of situations."

Velena took another sip of coffee and considered. "Yes, we all like at least the illusion of being in control. But maybe you're raising all these objections because you really can't tell." Velena raised her eyebrows in a challenge to Sara.

"You're sure? You've been warned."

"I'm sure," Velena said.

Sara leaned forward. "Did you ever cheat on your husband?"

Velena didn't change her cop poker face. "No," she said.

Sara shook her head. The scent was unmistakable. "Yes, you did."

Velena studied her. "Given statistics, you have about a 50/50 chance of being right."

"Then don't believe me. You don't have to."

Velena had gone somewhere in her mind — far away. Thinking. She spoke, almost to herself, "You would have made a good cop. Maybe when I turn in my badge, we can work together on a private case here and there."

They both finished their drinks and sat thinking. Then Velena asked, "So if you're right — what has Andersen been up to?"

"I have no idea," Sara said. "Which worries me."

Velena bit her lower lip. "I didn't read anything from him when he said no. But when you froze for a moment — I got tension from him then. I don't think he liked that at all. And he looked at you a couple of times later in the class. If you're right — you need to be careful."

"Don't worry. I don't leave home without my Rugar LC9."

"It won't do you much good in your purse."

Sara patted her chest, just under her bra. "It's right here."

"No!" Velena's jaw dropped. "I didn't see a thing — and I'm really careful about that. I need to know who's carrying and where."

Sara grinned. "You should check out this holster. It wouldn't work in a uniform — you need to have a loose-front shirt. But you just reach up under it and pull the gun down. And you can pack 2 extra mags in it too!"

Velena's eyes widened. "And nothing shows."

"I'll send you the link if you give me your email. It's from Femme Fatale Holsters."

"Of course it is."

They both laughed.

Velena looked at her watch. "Got to run," she said.

"Of course," said Sara, getting up.

They walked out of Joe's Joe and to the parking lot.

Velena reached out her hand to shake. "It's been interesting," she said.

Sara just nodded and shook hands.

"About the other thing," said Velena. "It's a long story that really isn't your business."

"You're right," said Sara.

# THREE

Sara always felt good walking into her home. First, her wolf-dog Skidi was there to greet her as though she were the most important person in the world. She loved that about dogs. Second, she had enough security devices in the house — including cameras that watched the street in both directions — that she could really relax here.

The deep breath she exhaled let her know just how not-relaxed she'd been out in the world.

She really liked Velena and the evening showed her how much she missed having a woman friend to talk to. But being home — feeling her neck and shoulder muscles relax — made her realize why she'd avoided making friends.

Over the past year, she had become afraid of cops. Afraid of them learning what she was. Afraid of being locked up.

She shook her head to clear it. A slab of steak for her and Skidi was would be perfect. She threw in some *pommes frites* for herself — although her French mom would have been horrified she made the fries out of yams instead of potatoes.

She sighed and let go of the familiar pain of missing her mom. Twenty years later and Sara still wanted to talk to her.

Tummy sated, she kicked off her cowboy boots and climbed into her brown leather recliner chair — which was big enough for Skidi to jump up beside her. She threw a Pendleton blanket over both of them.

Then Sara took out her cell — the protected one that supposedly even the NSA couldn't tap into — and called her computer geek friend Mason Spencer in central Pennsylvania. She'd rescued Mason about a year ago from people who wanted to kill him for what he found hacking their computers.

Ever since she rescued him, Mason wanted to help her. To be "on her team." And somehow — despite wanting to protect him — she'd let that happen. The man was just too valuable to the kind of missions she kept getting into.

And... heck, his enthusiasm was hard to resist.

She gave him Andersen's name and details and told him she suspected a serious felony there. Recent.

The next day, Mason told her he couldn't find anything suspicious about Andersen. He'd hacked his email accounts — personal and for the university. He'd found a modest bank account and nothing to suggest hidden money. If Mason couldn't find anything, Sara wasn't going to.

It should have reassured her. But she remained uneasy.

Mason gave her Andersen's home address, and Sara spent the next week watching it. Each night she saw Andersen return home around dinner time and not leave the rest of the night.

Maybe his felony was something non-violent — like tax evasion?

Two weeks later, Sara had finished the class with Andersen and moved to firearms training — another 32 hours in order to have an *armed* P.I. license. It made no sense. In Oklahoma, you don't need a license to carry a firearm — either concealed or right out in the open. So why would you need extra training to add something you could do anyway?

That class was taught by a different professor, so she no longer saw Andersen. She didn't see Velena in class anymore, either, as firearms training was excused for police officers.

Sara finished the class, passed the test, and got her P.I. license. Andersen slipped from her mind.

About a month after her talk with Velena, Sara signed into *Tulsa World Online* for her usual morning news fix and saw this lead story — "Decorated Police Detective Killed in Line of Duty."

Velena Davis's smiling face accompanied the article.

# FOUR

Sara was stunned.

Tulsa World Online said detectives Davis and Clete Bailey went to investigate a reported shooting and were instead ambushed. Davis heroically pushed Bailey aside but was gunned down by assailants who fled.

Sara left her computer and walked into the living room. She curled up in her leather recliner and patted her chest for Skidi to jump up and join her. She wrapped her arms around the dog.

It was so unfair. Nineteen years on the force and Velena had never been shot. In another year, she would have left the force — safe to enjoy the rest of her life.

And why the hell did it have to be Velena? In the past year, Sara had met a number of people who deserved to die. And others who are just taking up space in the world. Why must a woman who was doing good — helping people — have to die?

And — worst thought of all — did it have anything to do with whatever Greg Andersen was up to? Was it a coincidence that Velena's death came one month after she talked to Sara? Had she been looking into Andersen?

Sara got up and went back to her computer to learn more.

Police Chief Myron Willis was quoted saying this was an intolerable attack on a detective who devoted her life to protecting the people of Tulsa — and an attack on the police department itself.

There were quotes of shock from Velena's two adult children, Reginald Davis, age 34, a musician, and Nia Davis, an attorney with the Tulsa D.A.'s office.

Three days later Sara found herself on the streets of Tulsa, watching Velena's funeral procession. She saw Velena's sleek white hearse move from the All Souls Church under a huge American flag suspended over the road by two cranes, one on each curb.

Sara brushed away tears, and tried to understand the mess of feelings she experienced. She was sad, but there was something else too. Something... yes... she felt guilty.

But Velena never said she'd investigate. She never came back to Sara about the matter. For all Sara knew, Velena had brushed the idea aside because of all the "real" cases she had stacked on her desk.

Sara, herself, had brushed it aside.

Sara knew there was just a nano chance that Anderson was involved. But... if Velena died because of what Sara told her — Sara owed it to her to find out. To do otherwise would be unthinkable.

She pictured one day meeting Velena in the afterlife and trying to explain why she did nothing about the man who had killed her. Hell no. Sara wouldn't be able to live with herself unless she made sure Andersen was not involved.

Decision made, Sara returned home and googled the Tulsa police department — to find out who Velena's supervisor was. Google only listed the police chief's name and said there were two captains who together ran the detective division. But she got nowhere finding their names.

Her friend Mason got into the police department's emails for her. He found two detectives with the title of Captain — George Thatcher and Foster Protich. He ran checks on both of them — deep checks — but could find nothing suspicious in their emails. He ran financial checks, too — neither man had hidden bank accounts or more money than would be expected.

Mason also looked into Velena's two children. Reggie was an established jazz saxophonist who played clubs across the nation with a band called Rage for Life. Daughter Nia Davis had done the expected stint with the D.A. after getting her law degree, but unlike others, she never left for a big law firm. She stuck with the D.A.'s office and had moved up to Assistant D.A. She hadn't married.

"She could have moved to a big salary with a law firm," Mason told Sara. "She was in the top 5% of her law school, and she's got a good track record of winning cases. I think she was following in her mom's footsteps. Trying to protect people by putting away the bad guys."

"I'm frustrated," Sara told Mason. "We don't know if Velena and her partner were just in line for the next call, or if someone specifically assigned her to go to that location. If she was just next up, then it has nothing to do with Andersen."

"Well..." said Mason, "Clete Bailey's promotion is a big fat second coincidence."

"What promotion?"

"It's in your *Tulsa World* this morning. He was just moved from Robbery to Major Crimes."

"Major Crimes is a promotion?"

"I Googled "plum assignments police departments" and got that Major Crimes and Homicide are the two most prestigious units for detectives."

Sara thought. "If he was robbery before, why was he on that assignment with Velena? I thought she was in Homicide."

"She was," said Mason.

"And... why would you promote a man whose last assignment got his partner killed — and he didn't get the bad guy?"

"The announcement came from the Police Chief."

"Yeah, but I don't think he would have made the decision to promote Bailey," said Sara. "If he did that, he'd be meddling in how the captains run their detective division. That would really tick them off — and call a lot of attention to the promotion."

There was silence on the phone. Mason finally said, "You need to talk to a detective on this — but you can't. If your suspicion is right — the person you talk to could be in on it. Or if they're not — they could get killed investigating. I started a run on this Bailey. Maybe that will dig up something."

"I hope," said Sara. "We need to tie somebody there to Andersen — or I'm completely wrong about this."

Sara hung up. She wanted to be wrong, but her gut was screaming she wasn't.

# FIVE

Mason found nothing on Bailey. He told Sara, "Bailey doesn't have any personal connection with either of the two captains or with Andersen. And there's nothing fishy in his personal and work emails. Or bank accounts."

Sara spent the next day trying to get inspiration — but she was flat out of it. The only cops she knew on the force were the two others who'd been in P.I. school with her — that big slab of beef whose name she couldn't recall and Mike Walsh. She tried to imagine getting the needed information from Mike. He'd be jumping all over her from the first question. He could be in on it — although she didn't want to believe that. Or he could start investigating himself and end up dead like Velena.

The only path forward she could see would be talking to Velena's daughter Nia. At least she wouldn't jump in blindly and try to investigate like a cop.

But... how to broach her mother's death while she's grieving? "Oh, sure," she said to Skidi. "No problem. What could possibly go wrong?"

The next afternoon, Sara was back on the phone with Mason,

telling him her decision. Mason yelled at her for five full minutes, a very creative, curse-filled rant — including "dog vomit" and several Lupiti words she could only guess at. He concluded with "damn fool idea!"

Which, of course, it was.

When he finally ran down, Sara said, "You're right, it's crazy. But I just can't let it go. Also, I can't meet with her. She's grieving and probably angry, and it would be very satisfying to take out her pain on some conspiracy idiot intruding on her. But I think it could work as an email."

Reluctantly, Mason finally agreed to help her. They worked the wording, and that evening Nia's personal email received the following message:

---

*You don't know me, but I met your mother a month before she died. I really liked her, and you have my sympathies for your very great loss. At the time, your mother and I kicked around the idea of a person we knew being a probable felony suspect. While the odds of this having anything to do with her death are probably 99.9% against it, I find myself worrying about it and wanting to make sure.*

*I've investigated myself, but I've run into a dead end. To go further, I need the answers to these three questions:*

*1. Could either (or both?) of the detective captains assign her to a specific case? Anyone else?*

*2. Did she have a partner at work, and if so — who was it?*

*3. Did she talk in the last month with you about any case she was on? Maybe a side case she was looking into independently?*

*Please do not discuss this with anyone at all. Your mother was a smart, careful, suspicious woman — and if my fears are right she trusted the wrong person.*

*I'm going to be even more careful, which is why I'm*

*contacting you anonymously. There may even be someone in your office involved.*

*Yes, I know how paranoid this all makes me sound. But Velena is dead. Let me make sure it is what they say it is. Just in case it is not.*

*Please go to the following website — using the ID and password listed below. Give me your three answers, with as much detail as possible on the third question.*

*I will get back to you — within three weeks at the latest. I'll either tell you my fears were mistaken or I'll tell you what I learned.*

*I'm sorry to hit you with this at this time. But I believe you'll want to know as much or more than I do.*

*—Call me worried*

---

Sara found herself bingeing on Tums and Alka Selster as she waited for a response.. Mason assured her the private website couldn't be tracked and would disappear after Nia Davis responded. If she did.

On the third day, this message appeared on the website:

---

*1. Her captain Foster Protich is the only one who would assign her to something specific.*

*2. Her long-term partner Herman Rodriguez retired last year. Her partner for the last six months is Mike Walsh. But mom said Walsh was thinking about leaving the department.*

*3. She didn't tell me about any side projects*

*4. If I don't hear from you before day 22, I will use all the power of the Tulsa D.A.'s office and my police friends to find you and make you wish you'd never been born. AND at that time, you will damn well meet with me and answer all my questions.*

"You can't blame her," Mason said.

"I don't — in fact I like her for the threat. But I was really hoping she knew if her mom was investigating Andersen on the side."

Mason said he would keep trying to dig more into Protich. "But if he's hiding money, he's better at it than anyone I know — including security people. Ditto with Andersen."

# SIX

Sara had no remaining leads and nowhere to look for any more. But her gut kept insisting that Velena's death was Sara's fault — because she put Velena onto Andersen.

Finally, Sara broke down did the one thing she most wanted to avoid — call Mike Walsh. If he was in on it — great. Let him come after her. She was angry enough to tear him and anyone else involved to pieces. But if he wasn't... she'd have to figure some way to protect him if he started investigating like Velena did.

Sara's excuse for calling Mike was to ask if he was serious about starting a P.I. business. If so — she wanted to talk to him about it.

Unfortunately, he picked Joe's Joe for their meet.

It was a mistake for Sara to come back to the place. The black walls, the warm wood tones everywhere, the generous white coffee mugs — they all reminded her of Velena Davis. Of the friend she might have become.

Sara took a seat as far as she could get away from where she'd sat with Velena, but it didn't help her sadness. When she saw Mike enter the door, she waved him over. *Don't get him killed too*, said her brain.

Boy was she a bundle of sunshine.

Mike shook her hand with a smile on his face. Sara shook herself mentally and tried to focus on Mike. She'd forgotten how attractive he was. Not so much in looks — she was never attracted to buzz haircuts. But in his attitude. He was eager and interested in things — almost puppy-like. Gung ho. He could turn on the cop eyes, but they weren't his default personality.

"Are you OK?" he asked, sprawling out a little on the padded, comfortable chair.

*Was he reading her mind?* Sara looked in question at him.

"Sorry. You don't have to talk about it. But I saw you through the window before coming in — and you really looked sad."

*Just jump right into it,* she told herself.

"I was thinking about Velena Davis. We had coffee in this place after one of our P.I. classes. I really liked her."

Mike's face fell. "She was a good woman."

They both sat there in silence. A waitress stopped at their table with a big smile. Mike ordered a giant plain-black coffee and Sara an iced green tea latte — no sweetener.

The waitress picked up on the gloom at the table and hurried off to leave them alone.

"We were partners," Mike said. "These last six months, after her long-time partner retired. Best partner I've had. I was almost thinking about staying on longer."

"Why were you thinking of leaving?"

Mike looked down.

"Sorry," she added. "I didn't mean to be nosy. I just thought all cops stay in the job until they qualify for a pension."

Mike looked at her. Then he grimaced. "I found I stink at taking orders," he said. "And filling out forms. I wasn't called up for the military, so I had no idea how I'd react. I love solving crimes, but the piles and piles of paperwork..."

The waitress returned with their orders then left. Sara took a sip of her latte then nodded. "Much better than Starbucks."

Mike grabbed at the distraction. "A snob, huh? Why is it better?"

"For your information — in case you want to move up to a better drink than that swill..."

Mike raised one eyebrow.

"... Starbucks mixes sweetener in with the matcha powder. In their defense, most Americans hate unsweetened green tea — it's bitter."

"Let me taste it," he said.

"Nope. I learned my lesson. A very few people like me think it's the best thing they've ever tasted. Everyone else spits it out. I don't want you spitting it out and embarrassing me here."

Sara took another sip.

"Mike, if you were Velena's partner, why was she out with this Clete Bailey when she got shot?"

Mike's smile disappeared. "It was after shift. Bailey got a tip and his partner had left too. He pulled her in as backup."

"But Bailey's in robbery. Why would he ask her?"

Mike looked at her with eyes turned from warm to cop. "The tip said there was a body."

Sara waited for more, but Mike had stopped talking.

Sara just had to know. So she threw away caution and asked, "Then why did Bailey get promoted to Major Crimes?"

Mike looked at her intently. Finally he said, "You sent Nia the email, didn't you?"

# SEVEN

Sara couldn't help it — her eyes widened. She took a huge breath and let it out. This was a disaster.

"Nia talked to you about it?"

Mike nodded.

"Damn it, Mike." Sara was furious. "You're both asking to get killed. Nia was supposed to give me three weeks."

Mike's eyes narrowed. Softly, angrily, he said, "I'm a cop. She's a D.A. Who the hell are you?"

Sara looked around — grateful nobody was within earshot of them. She leaned forward. "I'm unknown, that's who I am. That's why I'm the person to do this."

She sat back in the chair and clamped her lips to prevent a scream of frustration. She leaned forward and said, "You do realize a cop has to be in on this? An upper-rank cop?"

Sara stood up. *The idiots!* She looked around again. Half the people in the restaurant were looking at her. She dug in her purse and threw some money on the table. She looked at Mike, shook her head, and walked out the door.

In her peripheral vision, she saw Mike also get up and follow her.

Sara stomped down the sidewalk, crossed a street to the parking lot, and got in her F150 truck. Mike ran up to her driver's side window and knocked on it. Sara stared at him. Then she unlocked the passenger side door and pointed at the seat.

He looked surprised, but after thinking about it she saw him nod. He circled the truck and got in. Sara looked around carefully. The lot was half full of mostly trucks, some cars. None were parked closer than 15 feet, and she saw nobody sitting in any of them.

She squeezed her leather-wrapped steering wheel as if she could bend it. She faced Mike.

"Do you even know what I'm worried about? Why it might have gotten Velena killed? Or are you and Nia just bumbling around in the dark?"

"Hey, lady, I got 10 years on the force." He was getting hot.

"Good for you. Velena had almost 40 — and she's still dead."

"She was my partner. I can't leave it alone." There was a croak in Mike's voice.

They stared at each other.

Mike added, "You wouldn't leave it alone either — if you were me."

Sara slapped both her palms on her face, covering her eyes. Rubbing them. She moved her hands up, running her fingers through her hair. She looked at him, anger evaporating.

"You're right," she conceded. "You're right."

"So what's your involvement in this?" he asked.

Sara shook her head. "First answer me this, was she working on a side investigation? Something on her own?"

"Yes."

"Do you know what it was?" Sara could see Mike wanted to be asking — not answering — questions. But he reconsidered and answered.

"No," he said. She could smell it was the truth.

"My 'involvement' in this," she said, "is I think I gave her the idea for her side investigation. If so, I got her killed. And now, by sending that email to Nia, I'm likely to get both of you killed as well."

"Thanks for your opinion of my skills," he said.

"Are they better than Velena's?"

"No. But I can guarantee you I'm going to be much more cautious."

"And Nia?"

"Let's make sure." Mike pulled out his phone and dialed a number on speed dial.

"It's me," he said. "I have someone you need to meet. Can you get away?"

Mike listened, then said, "Now would be best." He nodded to the phone and added, "Nowhere public."

Sara touched his arm. "Tell her to meet us at Lupiti Lake."

"That's 30 minutes away!"

"Exactly. And we can see anyone for two miles in all directions."

Mike nodded.

# EIGHT

Lupiti Lake spanned 250 acres, with five miles of shoreline. Sara and Mike met Nia's car at the main entrance, then they drove around to the virtually unpopulated side and parked.

There was a fishing area about a mile and a half away, and they could see two men in a decrepit fishing boat — casting. A mile in another direction, there were two beat-up campers in the camping area, and a couple of families sitting around a campfire. Nobody else was on the lake except a flock of grebes, bobbing on the water — their gray bodies highlighted by the white neck patches that run up to just under their eyes.

Sara refused to talk near Nia's car, assuming it could be compromised. Instead they crammed into Sara's F150 truck.

Sara's first words to Nia were, "I can't tell you how pissed I am you talked to someone about this."

Nia shot back, "Pissed back at you. You sent that letter without giving me a chance to participate. Who the hell do you think you are — the Lone Ranger?"

Sara tried to calm down. "I'm someone who feels guilty about your mother dying — and who doesn't want more dead people to feel guilty about."

"And," she continued, "Yes, I am used to operating like the Lone Ranger. I'm used to helping people who can't help themselves. I admit, you two aren't like them.

"But... neither was your mother, damn it. *I liked her.* She'd want to kill me for getting you involved."

They sat there in silence. Mike finally broke it. "How about a truce? We're in it now, so what do we do from here?"

Sara rubbed her eyes again. "You're right."

So Sara told them the whole story. The class, the teacher Greg Andersen, her coffee chat with Velena. She didn't tell them how she convinced Velena she could smell a lie — just that she did.

Nia and Mike sat there for a minute, both looking stunned.

"That's it?" Nia asked, incredulously. "Just his reaction to your question about a 'recent felony'?"

Mike shook his head, slowly. "Not entirely," he said. "Andersen had a real reaction to Sara. But I thought he was just annoyed at a student one-upping him."

Sara nodded. "That was there too."

Nia asked Sara, "So what exactly do you do?"

Answering questions like this was why Sara got the private investigator license.

"I'm a P.I.," she said. "I was functioning as one before, but now I'm licensed. I help people. But I'm in this because your mother died — and I think Andersen's involved."

Mike opened the door and got out. "I need to breathe," he said.

Sara and Nia got out too. They walked the 10 feet to the water. A light breeze was stirring, making ripples on the lake. Mike picked up a stone and skipped it, getting three bounces.

"So..." Nia started to say, but Sara turned her away from the water.

"Humor me," she said. "Just in case we were followed, and someone who can read lips is over there with binoculars."

Nia raised her eyebrows, but she nodded. All three turned 180 from the lake.

"So..." Nia continued, "you have a tech guru who's been digging into Andersen? And he's found nothing?"

"Nothing thus far on phones, emails, or bank accounts," Sara said. "And before you ask, my guy is good. Really good."

There was confusion in the silence that followed.

"And," said Sara, "I watched Andersen's home for a week. The guy doesn't leave his house."

Mike said, "I think that's what Velena was doing. Tailing him. Watching his house. She was putting in some long, boring hours. She was tired all the time."

Nia asked, "You think he saw her?"

"Or somebody else did," Sara agreed. "Another watcher. Or a camera."

Mike pursed his lips. "If this is right — if we're not inventing the whole thing — then Clete Bailey is probably in on it."

Sara said, "He almost has to be. And there has to be another cop in on it — senior to Bailey. Because Bailey didn't do this on his own. I'm guessing it's whoever promoted him after."

"George Thatcher promoted him," said Mike.

"That's weird," said Sara. "It's unlikely he and Protich could both be dirty, isn't it?"

Mike nodded.

"Maybe..." Nia said, "Maybe if Andersen doesn't leave the house — then whatever he's doing is in there. He doesn't have to go out."

All three looked at each other. Mike nodded. "It's worth a look."

"I'll have my tech get house plans," said Sara. "And Andersen's teaching schedule — when he'll be out of the house."

"Just don't plan anything without me," Nia said.

Sara looked at both of them. "Ground rules," she said. "Only my tech looks into Thatcher, Andersen and Bailey. We should assume they're watching Mike's computers — and probably Nia's as well."

They both nodded.

Mike said, "If we don't find anything — we stop this. Admit there's nothing here that could have caused Velena's death. Hell, maybe she was investigating something else not related to this."

"Agreed," said Sara. Nia nodded.

# NINE

Mason got back to Sara on Sunday with Andersen's house plans and schedule, so Sara left a message for Mike and Nia. She told them to show up the next day separately at the Cinemark Broken Arrow movie theatre for a noon retrospective showing of the 1984 *Dune* movie.

As expected, there were few in the theatre. Sara sat with her back against the back wall. Mike arrived next.

"You couldn't have picked some nice shoot 'em up movie?" he asked. "I never got the point of this sci-fi crap."

"You and every other Tulsa male," Sara responded, rolling her eyes. "We're here because I didn't want a crowd."

Sara passed him the tub of popcorn. "No complaints about no butter," she said. "Because it's really butter-flavored rancid oil. If you want that, you can go get your own."

Mike tapped his chest. "Hey, this body is a temple. I protect it."

"Yeah, yeah," she said, smiling.

Two minutes later, Nia arrived with red eyes — she looked like she'd been crying. She grabbed the popcorn tub out of Mike's hands and sat down, popping one kernel in her cupid bow mouth.

"Are you alright?" asked Mike.

"Let's make it quick," Nia said. "I have two assholes lined up after lunch that need reaming out."

OK, thought Sara, *if that's how she wants to play it.*

Sara smiled. "Great to see you too, Nia."

"Bite me."

"I pass."

"Hey," Mike said. "I'm willing."

Both women rolled their eyes.

"OK," said Sara. "Here's what we've got. First, my tech went into the school records and finally found one tiny connection between Andersen and a captain — but it's not Thatcher. Protich recommended Andersen for the teaching job. So they had to know each other at least well enough for that."

There were identical raised eyebrows from Nia and Mike. Sara smothered a smile.

"Second, Andersen is again teaching that P.I. class Mike and I went to — both tomorrow and Thursday night. It lasts from 6:30 to 8:30. Given 15-20 minutes travel time each way, that will give us from about 6:10 until 8:45. Let's do it Thursday as it will give us some time to prepare."

Sara looked at Mike and Nia, and both nodded.

"We certainly don't need three people inside, so Nia... we really need a lookout."

"No," said Nia. "It's my mom. And don't worry about me — I'm a cop's daughter. I was firing a gun from the day I was born."

Sara looked at Mike, who shrugged. Sara sighed. "OK, looks like I'll need to get a couple of night vision cameras to replace Nia as lookout. And I'll bring a satellite map and some wireless headsets — so my tech can keep in contact with us. It's best we don't bring any police equipment. They could be watching."

Mike was looking at Sara with a thoughtful expression.

"What?" she asked.

"You *have* been doing this before."

"Well, duh!"

Mike said, "Why do I get the feeling you don't want us with you? You want to cowboy it."

"Play nice, you two," said Nia.

The three of them agreed to meet at a local mall parking lot at 5PM on Thursday. Mike and Nia got up and left.

Sara looked up at the movie screen. She *did* like this "sci-fi stuff" but she remembered this old *Dune* movie as a dog — nothing like the good one in 2021. She left too.

# TEN

The very next night — Tuesday — Sara pulled up in her truck and parked about a mile from the Andersen home. Nia and Mike would hate her guts when they found out she went in without them. But this should be a simple in-and-out. If it wasn't — she was better able to survive an encounter with an armed someone.

And she was damned if she was going to get another person killed.

She walked towards the back of the house, thin latex gloves on, carrying a bag and a soccer ball. She stuck a night vision camera on a tree facing the back of Andersen's house. Then she circled the house and put another on a telephone pole facing the house entrance.

Facing his house, Sara thought once again it was a strange choice for a glossy ladies man like Andersen. It looked like a house his mom might have lived in, long after she was able to keep it up. White brick, dark brown trim, and roof. Scraggly yard and dead flower beds.

Records showed it *was* his mom's — Andersen inherited it after her death. It was a warning flag to Sara that he didn't sell it and put the money into some chrome condo more his style.

What it did have was some isolation. The houses on this street were set back 15-25 feet from the road. The neighbors on one side of Andersen's house were 50 feet away, 30 feet away on another side. Behind his house was an empty lot.

She checked in with Mason via her earbud, who confirmed he was getting clear visuals from both of the cameras.

"I don't like this," Mason told her for the nine hundredth time. "I understand protecting Nia. But Mike could hold his own. You should have brought him. I think you're avoiding him because you're attracted to him."

"Excuse me?"

"When was the last time you got laid? Bet you can't even remember that far back."

"You want to talk about my sex life? *Now?* Maybe we should talk about yours? Or... gee... here's an idea. Maybe we should instead talk about how I'm about to break into a bad guy's house?"

Sara shook her head and grouched. "You're not my mom. Now shut up — I'm going in."

# ELEVEN

Facing the house front, Sara took out the soccer ball and threw it towards the front door. It hit the door jamb and bounced back on the dirt about six yards out. No audible sirens sounded. Not a single light went on.

Sara walked to the door, John Deere baseball cap pulled down to cover her face from any cameras. There were two deadbolt locks on the door — a Yale and a Schlage.

Sara knew she couldn't pick them. She couldn't believe all the movies and novels that had people easily picking locks. She wasn't sure anyone could actually pick a lock. It might all be lies.

Last year Sara bought a lock picking kit, where you could see the tumblers inside the lock. Even with the instructions, she couldn't do it. She'd wasted hours and hours — days even — trying to master it. She eventually pounded the lock into tiny pieces with a hammer before throwing it away.

She took the night vision camera from her lapel and pointed it all around the door, taking time in the eaves. Mason told her over her headset that he couldn't see any cameras.

"Two deadbolt locks, but no lights and no cameras? It doesn't make sense."

Sara moved around the side of the house to where someone driving by wouldn't see her. Another camera check found nothing. Sara put on her night vision goggles and checked the window carefully. It was frosted, like it might be a bathroom window. There was no security tape on it wired to an alarm system.

She pulled out a roll of wide black electrical tape — stickier than duct tape — and covered the bottom pane of the window, pressing hard. She took a glass cutter and cut a circle in the bottom corner, big enough for an arm. She tapped the glass inside the circle and heard it break. Then she pulled off the tape, and the circle of now-broken glass came with it.

Her arm went carefully inside the hole and Sara opened the window clasp. She raised the window, then stood there listening. She heard nothing.

She re-clipped the camera for Mason securely to her jacket and climbed in the window. She was in a small room with just a sink and a toilet. Old-fashioned wallpaper on the walls.

Sara needed to clear the house. She walked to the door, listened carefully, then exited, her Rugar LC9 leading the way. She had just checked to her left — clear — when she finally noticed her wolf brain screaming at her.

Man smells!

# TWELVE

A pistol touched her right temple. Wow! It was something she'd experienced just once before, and hadn't wanted to experience it ever again. The cold steel made her stomach cramp and her breath stop.

She wasn't sure even a werewolf could recover from having her brains blown out. She didn't want to test it. Ever.

Sara tensed. Her right hand could move fast — hit the gun aside — as her left gun hand could turn towards the man. Or play for time? He hadn't shot her yet. Maybe he would be stupid enough to want to talk?

Sara took a careful breath, then startled at the scent she pulled in. When was she ever going to learn to "look" first with her nose? Before her eyes.

"Hi Mike," she said. "You planning to shoot me? Was it something I said?"

She felt him freeze. He took the gun from her temple. He pushed on her right shoulder to turn her facing him. Sara brought her gun around with the turn — pointing it straight at him.

They stared at each other and at the guns each had aimed at the other. They seemed frozen.

Mike blinked first, then jerked his gun up, away from her. Sara pointed hers down.

"Now who's cowboying it?" she asked.

The right side of Mike's mustache pulled down. "Both of us, apparently," he said.

"How long have you been in?"

"About 10 minutes. I've cleared it. Nobody's here."

Sara looked at Mike's hands. Yes, he was wearing thin gloves like hers. Mike noticed her look.

"I'm not an idiot," he said.

Sara winced. "I know. But I'm guessing the police aren't typically sneaking into someone's house worried about leaving fingerprints. At least, I hope not."

"And you are?"

Sara ignored the question.

"Let me and M... my tech see this place," Sara said. She was not going to use Mason's name in front of a cop.

She searched the house quickly, letting Mason look via the camera at the ceilings, pictures and mirrors. The house looked like Andersen's mom still lived here. The kitchen had appliances so old they could have been in a '50s or '60s museum — except for a new, shiny refrigerator. Laminate was everywhere — the counters a hideous mottled green that looked like mold even though it wasn't.

A rickety old table with years of peeling paint was shoved against the wall. It had a moth-eaten rag rug under it, like you used to see in old country kitchens on TV. The table had just one chair at it. Guess Andersen wasn't cooking for guests. From the looks of it, he wasn't cooking at all.

The master bedroom still had frilly mom drapes on the windows, although the chenille bedspread that belonged with them was gone. Plain sheets and a blanket covered the bed. There was an ornate dark brown wood dresser.

Mike was right. Nobody was home.

Mike paged through the master closet, shaking his head. "Andersen's living in this dump — but spending my entire salary on clothes."

They moved to a bedroom serving as an office. Sara sat in front of the computer so Mason could see it through the camera.

"Wow," he said in her ear. "That looks like a Mac Plus from about 1990. It still works?"

"Let's see," Sara said, moving to switch it on.

"Stop!"

Sara's hand froze.

Mason said, "It could be booby-trapped to send up an alarm. Let me see the back."

Sara moved the camera all around the computer, but Mason saw nothing.

Sara turned it on.

It booted up, and she saw a home page pop up with Safari. "Wow," she heard in her ear. "It's been refurbished. It looks like they..."

There was a rush of geek-speak in her ear, but Sara tuned it out. Instead, she looked at the browsing history. Andersen had visited Gateway First Bank, *Tulsa World Online*, and a number of police websites.

Mike looked at the screen, then showed her a checkbook from the drawers. It showed a $1,283.43 balance in the checking.

"There's nothing here," Mike said. "We should leave."

Sara looked at her watch. It was 7:42 PM. The earliest Andersen could return would be 8:45. Unless he cut the class short for some reason.

"There's just not enough here," she said, frustrated. "Nobody leads a life this bland. This empty. What's he do with his time? His money?"

In her ear, Mason said, "He's got a savings account at the same bank. He opened it with $60,000 right after his mom died. He's been slowly using the money. Maybe $10K a year. That, plus the $15K he's making from the police. No rent or mortgage. He can live on it."

She told Mike. "He could live on it," Mike agreed. "Barely."

"But is he?" she asked. "What's your cop sense telling you?"

Mike looked at her. "Not with those clothes. But there's no answer here."

"You should leave," Sara agreed.

"What are you going to do?"

"I'm going to take a half-hour and be really weird. Just to make sure."

Mike tilted his head. He smoothed down his mustache. "I'll stay and watch you get weird."

# THIRTEEN

"Stay at least 15 feet away from me," Sara told Mike. "I'm going to use my sense of smell."

She turned and walked to the back of the house — not wanting to see whatever look that got out of Mike.

She started in the laundry room, between the kitchen and the back door. It wasn't large — just enough room for a fat chipped-white Sears washer and dryer and the two doors. She stood in the middle of the space and closed her eyes, and inhaled. She smelled Mike.

She opened her eyes and saw him in the kitchen doorway. "Back up," she told him. "Stand back 15 feet at least. All I can smell is you."

His eyes went wide, but he backed up to the other side of the kitchen, standing where he could still see her.

She tried again. If only Mike had left — she could transform and get her full wolf nose to work. But maybe, even as a human...

She inhaled through her nose. Soap. Old pizza. Rodents — mice, not rats. She lifted her nose up towards the attic. Nothing different. She squatted down closer to the floor. Same smells. And dirt. Nothing.

She moved into the kitchen, backing Mike out into the hall. More food smells. More mice. Garbage. She lifted her nose up towards the ceiling. She squatted down on the floor. Nothing unusual.

This was stupid. There was just no real point without using her wolf nose. And probably no real point even then.

Sara just found it hard to believe her gut instinct was wrong. She twisted on her ankles to see Mike — to see how weird he thought she was acting — when she froze. There was just the slightest hint of something. A molecule of scent taunting her.

Was it really there? Or was she that desperate to justify her instincts? Only one way to find out.

"Stay back," she said. "Way back. It might be nothing."

The floor was disgusting, but she kneeled on it. Put her hands down on it. Even her elbows. She put her nose about 2 inches from the floor. The smell she was seeking wasn't here. She slowly turned a full circle. Nothing.

She remembered the direction she'd been facing when she noticed the scent and crawled towards the old table. Nothing. She crawled on top of the rag rug and completely under the table. She smelled the wall under the table. Nothing.

She looked at her watch. It was 8:10 — time to get out of here.

She crawled out from under the table. Angrily she lifted the corner of the rag rug. And there was the smell after all. Just a wisp of smell. But unmistakable. A sex smell. Old semen. Under the rug. Under the table.

# FOURTEEN

Sara stood quickly and jerked the table and rug away from the wall. The floor had a trap door. An old one, nothing new. But it had new weather stripping all around holding back any smells — and noises?

"Holy shit," Mike said softly, suddenly right beside her.

"I'll bet it was a root cellar," she said.

"Let's see what it is now." He grabbed the rounded handle and pulled it. The door swung up on a hinge. There was a ladder down to what looked like a dirt floor.

Mike turned as though to start down the stairs. Sara grabbed his arm.

"Not yet," she said. He reluctantly nodded, then he pulled back. Or tried to. He looked at her hand, holding his arm. He frowned, wondering why he couldn't pull it away.

*Oops*, she thought and let go of his arm. Sometimes she forgot her new strength.

Quickly she touched her headset.

"Tech? You see?"

"Yes," said Mason. "What do you want me to do?"

"Keep a serious eye on the outside of this place. If you see anyone come in the house, and you can't reach me, call the cops and the media. Tell them about the room under the kitchen. We don't want to get trapped down there."

"Understood."

"I'm setting my watch for a 15-minute warning. If you don't hear from me and can't reach me before 20 minutes are gone — again alert everyone."

Sara looked at Mike. "I lead," she said. "My nose may be able to warn us."

Mike nodded.

Sara leaned over the edge of the hole and stuck her head down it. That same smell was here, just as faint. She smelled dirt, roots, dankness, and an aftertaste of Andersen. But no human was in this room. No body either. She turned on her flashlight.

It *was* a former root cellar. Dirt floor. An old metal set of shelves with jars so dusty you couldn't see inside them. The room was maybe six foot by eight.

Sara twisted her torso around. Back under the stairs, where you would be least likely to see it, was a door so covered with dirt it looked like it had been covered on purpose. It blended in with the walls, except for the shiny big padlock on it.

"OK so far," she said to Mike, then climbed down. The ceiling was low, old boards. It scrapped the top of her 5'7" head. Mike climbed down and joined her. He couldn't stand up without bending his knees.

Sara stared at the padlock. She looked everywhere, hoping for a key. But there wasn't one.

"We're screwed," she said.

"Don't tell me you can't pick a lock?"

"Don't tell me you can," she said. "Nobody can pick locks. It's something they make up in the movies."

Mike shook his head with pity at her. "How do you think I got in this house?"

"Prove it."

Mike grinned at her and pulled out a set of pick tools, knelt by the padlock and started to work. He expertly inserted a rake pick, turned it, and then inserted a triangle pick.

"So how did you get in the house?" he asked, his eyes unfocused as he concentrated on touch.

"Through a window," she mumbled.

"Through a window," he repeated, focused on the lock. "But all the windows were locked." His hands froze, and he looked at her.

"Don't tell me you broke the glass?"

"OK, I won't."

A grin as wide as the Cheshire Cat's split Mike's face. "So that was the noise I heard."

Sara tried distraction. "So how long is this going to take you?"

Sara heard a disturbing metal click and the lock popped open.

"How's that?"

Sara stared at the lock. "I can't believe it!"

Mike pocketed his picks and rubbed his fingers on each hand with his thumbs. "Talented fingers," he said, smirking.

"Yeah, yeah." But she was laughing.

Then both of their smiles disappeared. Sara sniffed hard at the door. But the smells she got were the same as those in the root cellar.

She opened the door. Behind it was a tunnel — a long tunnel. Maybe 35 yards. The first 10 yards or so looked like it was built when the root cellar was. The rest of the tunnel looked new. It had plywood ceilings and propped-up beams holding it up. Nobody was in it.

There was a green garden extension cord hanging from the ceiling, all along the tunnel. Bare light bulbs hung every 10 feet or so. There was a switch at the entrance. Sara pointed to it and said to Mike, "Let's not, OK?"

Mike nodded. Their flashlights were sufficient. And who knew if the switch worked the lights or was a signal. Or both.

"Tech? We're going into a tunnel." Sara heard a click of acknowledgment in her ear.

She and Mike walked down the tunnel. It felt claustrophobic

with just the moving flashlights breaking a blackness so complete you felt like you'd been buried deep in the earth. Which, of course, they were.

Sara tried Mason again, but there was no response. They were completely alone down here.

The tunnel ended in a door that was just like the one at the start of it.

"It's got to be the house next door," Mike whispered in Sara's ear. "I never looked into it. Did you?"

"No," she whispered back. "Ma... Tech looked into the surrounding houses but only to see if Andersen owned them. He didn't."

"Or," she considered, "he doesn't own them under his name."

"You going to sniff the door for us? See if anyone's there?"

Sara shined her flashlight into Mike's face. He was smirking.

"Hey!" He put his hand over the light.

"Yes, I am," she said. "And I'm going to listen at it. You're just jealous."

"I am. How do you do it?"

"Be quiet," she said and moved to the door. She listened but heard nothing — other than their breathing and their two hearts beating in the tunnel.

She put her nose to the door, closed her eyes from the flashlights, and inhaled.

"I'm only smelling Andersen here — nobody else. I think only he uses the tunnel. Whoever's up in this house stays there. That means I don't have a clue how many there are. So be prepared for anything."

"Agreed."

She motioned Mike closer. With his face almost touching hers, she said, "I'll go left." He nodded. They both turned off their flashlights and stored them in pockets.

Sara took the doorknob in her right hand. Her left held her Colt 1911, the barrel pointing chest high at where the door would open.

She jerked the door back towards them, swinging it open. She let go of the knob and moved into the room and to the left. Her right hand pulled out her Rugar LC9 from her front belly band holster. Mike passed her, moving to the right.

Total darkness. Sara inhaled through her nose. It was a cellar, and there was nobody in it besides them.

"Clear," she whispered. She replaced her Colt 1911 and took the flashlight back out. The beam revealed a similar setup to what they'd left behind at Andersen's house. And it showed Mike, shaking his head with a bemused grin.

"I can't believe I lowered my gun on your "clear" in a completely dark room!" he whispered.

Sara's light found the wood stairs leading up.

"Urgent, respond." It was Mason's voice in Sara's ear. She held up a hand to Mike.

# FIFTEEN

"I'm here," Sara whispered.

"Andersen's home," came Mason's voice in her earbud.

"He's entering his house right now. Five alive in this house — two huge, two small, one medium. One of the biggies is in the kitchen."

Sara's jaw dropped. How could he tell that all the way from Pennsylvania?

But she quickly relayed the info to Mike, who quietly closed the door to the tunnel. Sara carefully climbed the stairs — keeping her feet on the outside part of each — and pushed a little on the trap cellar door. No movement. She pushed harder and felt a very slight give. She climbed back down.

"They've got something heavy on it," she whispered. "We can't pretend to be Andersen. He for sure either calls them before coming or gives some kind of code knock. We'd be walking up into a gun."

"No quick way to get them out of the kitchen?" Sara asked Mason & Mike at the same time.

"I need 60 seconds," Mason said in her ear. "Be ready."

Immediately, Sara heard a phone ringing above them.

"Tech, you ringing the phone?" Sara hissed.

"No."

"Assume Andersen's calling upstairs," Sara told Mike.

The phone ringing was cut off. Someone had picked it up. Then Sara heard the doorbell ring above.

"Now's your best chance," Mason said in her ear. Sara heard hesitation and regret in his voice — but she didn't have time to question it.

Sara and Mike both climbed the stair and put shoulders to the trap door. Together they shoved hard. The trap door came up almost two feet, then suddenly got lighter as it continued to open.

A woman's loud voice from another room asked, "Where's Betty Sue? I damn well know she's in there."

*Oh, hell*, thought Sara, recognizing Nia's voice.

# SIXTEEN

A bang sounded as the table which had been on top of the cellar door tipped over and crashed to the floor.

A huge, steroid-pumped man dashed into the kitchen, gun coming up.

"Police," yelled Mike. His gun, which had been pointed back down the stairs to where Andersen was expected, started to rise.

The giant's pistol, which looked like a mini in his hand, kept coming up.

Sara shot him. She aimed for his gun hand which was moving up his right side. She'd either get the hand or his side — neither of which should be fatal. Either of which should stop him.

She got both. His gun dropped, and he fell back on the floor, screaming.

An arm holding an automatic pistol came around the kitchen door frame and sprayed the room with bullets.

Sara and Mike ducked back down the stairs — fast as they could.

The instant the firing stopped, Sara looked up and put her remaining seven bullets into the wall the new shooter had to be hiding behind. There was a muffled vocal sound and a thud that sounded like a body dropping to the floor.

She ducked back down immediately, told Mike she was out, grabbed another magazine from her corset holster, slammed it back in, and made sure nobody was coming through the tunnel door.

Mike was watching both the man on the floor, who was starting to move to where his gun had fallen, and the kitchen door.

"Cover me," Sara whispered, then climbed up, grabbed the man on the floor, zip-tied his remaining good hand to his ankle, and kicked the gun to the other side of the room.

"Tunnel's yours," she said to Mike, as she took over watching the doorway.

"Tech — status?" she said.

Over her earbud, she heard, "Nia's in the house. Andersen's getting in his car to escape."

Sara told Mike, whose eyes widened. He hadn't recognized Nia's voice.

She motioned for the two of them to step back down the stairs, heads below the floor level.

"Five in the house," she said. "One zip-tied here, another possible down behind the door frame."

"Three to four whereabouts unknown," said Mike. "And Nia's in the house. Let's see what's left."

"Kitchen is clear," yelled Sara.

A spray of bullets flew into the kitchen.

"Tech, don't lose Andersen," Sara said.

She and Mike both watched the kitchen doorway.

"Don't shoot. It's Nia."

Sure enough, Nia's head and body edged out into the doorway, a man's thick hairy arm wrapped around her shoulders, pinning her left visible arm. Her eyes were wide with fear.

"I got a gun aimed right at her head," said a high, squeaky man's voice that didn't match the arm. To prove it, Nia's head was pushed to the side until an automatic pistol came into view, mashed against her right temple. The man stayed hidden.

Nia was taking short, fast breaths. Sara could see her thinking — trying to find a way out of it. Sara recognized the look of a woman with courage and brains, but no physical training to back it up.

It was criminal that the U.S. school system didn't teach all girls hand-to-hand combat — from grade school through college. But they didn't.

Sara really wanted to put more bullets right through the wall and into the man holding Nia. But even if that happened to kill the man, he would still have time to kill Nia. The only shot that would drop him with no chance to fire would be if she could hit his Medulla Oblongata. A shot nobody could make without seeing the target.

Sara stood up. Mike grabbed her leg to stop her, but she shook her head at him. She extended a flat hand down at him, warning him to stay where he was. She hoped he wouldn't get all macho on her, but she was the one member of this team most likely to survive a bullet.

Not that she could tell him that. Not that she could explain there was no way that bullet would be made of silver.

"OK," said Sara, standing. "You got me. I'm putting down my gun. Just don't hurt her."

"Don't!" said Nia, horrified.

"How many are you?" asked the unseen man.

"It's just me," Sara said.

"I heard two guns."

"Both mine," said Sara. She looked quickly at Mike, who handed her the one he'd been using then pulled another from his ankle. Then he ducked down the stairs out of sight. Nia's eyes got even wider. She shook her head, warning Sara.

"Can we talk?" Sara asked. "I'll put both guns on the floor."

Nia was jerked back a little; then the man leaned his head out to look at the room, keeping carefully behind Nia's head. He only had to bend down a little, which made him maybe 5'9" max.

If Mason was right, there were still one huge guy and two smaller people — perhaps women — somewhere in the house. Unless she already killed the big guy when she behind the door?

"Sorry about your two friends," she said, hoping.

"Not my friends," he growled.

*OK*, she thought, standing there. She was holding a pistol in each hand, both raised in surrender.

"Put the guns on the floor," he rasped. "Slowly."

Sara lowered her hands slowly. She really, really wanted to have a shot, but the only things exposed behind Nia's head were a cheek and some overly gelled brown hair. He couldn't even see Sara to know if she was complying.

"Now! Or I blow her away and then get you."

*Damn. Damn. Damn.* Sara lowered her guns. She let them make an audible sound as their butts hit the floor, but she kept her hands on them — fingers on the triggers.

Nia watched Sara's hands. She took a deep breath. Then Nia cried, "I'm gonna be sick." She made a retching noise and started to bend at the waist as though to vomit. Her folding in the middle pulled the man behind her forward. Nia then threw herself towards the floor with all her weight, exposing the man's head.

Sara gasped at Nia. If the man had shot immediately, she would have been dead. *What was that woman thinking?*

Sara's right hand didn't care in the slightest what Nia was thinking. The minute Nia started to bend, Sara's right hand lifted the Rugar LC9 from the floor, pointed it directly between the man's eyes, and pulled the trigger. Hitting the Medulla Oblongata.

He collapsed right on top of Nia, who desperately shoved herself out from under him — making little whimpering noises.

The man had dropped the gun without firing a shot — just like Sara's research had said he would.

But without Nia making that move, Sara would have never risked her life on the shot.

# SEVENTEEN

Sara looked at Nia, shaking her head. "You idiot! Coming in here like you're Rambo!" She grabbed Nia's shoulders, shook her head at her, then crushed her in a hug.

Nia hugged her back, then pushed her away hard. "Don't start with me. You left me behind! Even though it's *my* mama."

Mike had bounded up the stairs. Quickly he checked the dead man, double-checked the wounded man, and grabbed all the loose guns. He handed one to Nia.

"I got words for you too," Nia said to Mike. He ignored her and ducked his head around the door and quickly back. Then he left the room. He sent an automatic pistol sliding back into the room. Sara grabbed it.

Mike re-emerged, dragging a very large, very dead body into the room. Sara had got the other guy after all.

"Yeah, well," Mike said as he slung the body over to the other dead man. "While you two are having girl bonding crap — someone has to remember there are two other possible hostiles in the damn house!"

Sara smiled. "You're right, Mike. Lead on. We'll follow. Just let me close the back door." Sara flipped the door back down and pulled the toppled table back on top of it. Nia helped her.

"One more thing," Nia said. Sara rolled her eyes. "Thanks for saving me."

"Anytime," said Sara. "And thanks for thinking fast. I *really* didn't want to let go of those guns."

"Great," said Mike sarcastically. "You're becoming BFFs. How sweet. Now can we check out the rest of the house?"

It was a big house for its age. Sara looked through the living and dining rooms, then checked the hall closet. There were three bedrooms that would have been for kids. Two looked like wild men lived in them — clothes everywhere and the ripe smell of unwashed everything. A third was being used by the smaller man. His closet had better clothes in it — and they were on actual hangers.

There was a bathroom that looked like ebola could be growing in it. Two linen closets with nothing much.

Just two rooms to go.

The door to the first one was locked. It had a front door Schlage lock on it, with the key in the lock. Mike motioned them to the sides of the door then he turned the key.

Hearing nothing, he opened the door and slammed it hard, so it bounced off the wall and came back. Inside were two twin mattresses on the floor on opposite sides of the room. A young woman was lying on each of them. The closet and the attached bathroom were both clear.

Both of the women were very young and very pretty, although one of them had serious bruising all over her arms and legs. Maybe more, under a cheap cotton dress. The woman was asleep and wouldn't wake up. Drugged probably. There were serious tracks on her bare feet and lower legs.

The other woman was awake but foggy. She shrunk away from them and covered her head with her arms. She wasn't showing any bruising, but she also had foot and leg track marks. Maybe half as many as the other girl.

Nia whipped out her phone and placed a call.

Mike and Sara looked at each other, then moved to the final unopened door, guns out.

Mike did the door-slamming thing again and the head ducking in and back out thing again. Then he walked in. Sara followed.

The room had been a very large family room. It was now a cheap movie studio. There were three "sets" around the room. A bedroom set was on one wall. Another had a toilet and tub against a tiled wall — with no plumbing. And there was a dungeon set — with what looked like a concrete block wall with manacles attached to it.

In the center of the room was some kind of sound console and a very serious computer setup. Two moveable cameras were parked by two of the sets.

"I'm calling the chief — telling him to come by himself," Mike said.

Sara nodded. "I'm going after Andersen."

She stopped at the door. "Mike, if you can, I would really like to have never been here."

He looked at her. "Are you sure? You broke this — you should get the credit."

Sara shook her head. "Don't want it."

He slowly nodded his head. "OK. But tell Nia on your way out."

"Thank you! I will."

# EIGHTEEN

Sara jumped in her F150 truck and started the engine. "Tell me you've got Andersen," she said over her earpiece to Mason.

"I've got him," Mason reassured her. "He headed straight downtown. Start driving, and I'll tell you where he stops."

Sara took turns then got on the freeway. She found she was furious, so she took two deep breaths before she said something she'd regret.

"Mason," she said, as calmly as she could. "How exactly did Nia show up at the house?"

Her earbud went silent.

"Mason..."

"I called her," he said.

"It took time for her to get there. When did you call her?"

"Right after you taped the window."

Sara said nothing.

Mason said, "I needed eyes on the ground. A person, not just cameras. Nobody was supposed to be in the house, but I had a bad feeling."

A car swerved into her lane, forcing Sara to slam on the brakes to avoid rear-ending it. Sara swore heatedly.

"Hey," Mason said, "I would never have called her if I thought she'd be in real danger."

"But you sent her into a house with five heat signatures?"

"Yes. I told her the danger, but she agreed to go in. And... it's a good thing I did."

"Yes, it is. You saved our butts. I hate it — you should know that. But you did the right thing."

By the time Sara got to downtown Tulsa, Mason reported that Andersen had parked on South Main Street and went into the Ambassador Hotel. Mason would let her know if Andersen left.

Sara made a quick stop at her downtown office — one large room plus bathroom in a high rise that also housed a shoe repair shop plus doctor and attorney offices, and which was across the alley from the back door of a good restaurant. In other words — hidden among other businesses that anyone might have a reason to visit.

The place was coming in more handy than she'd thought. She'd already used it to meet clandestinely with a new client. Now she used it to change her appearance. The all-black she was wearing was OK. She just added some low heels to replace the black boots and threw on a designer jacket. A red wig and big sunglasses completed the look and should protect her at least a little from camera surveillance.

Back in her car for the 20 or so blocks to the Ambassador Hotel, Sara asked Mason to update her.

Andersen hadn't left, so it appeared he was staying there. Sara asked for his room number, and was treated to another heart-felt string of cuss words. Mason was furious he couldn't get in, quickly, to the front desk system.

"I'll get in," he promised. "But it might take me another 30 minutes. Which is fricking ridiculous, because hotel systems are always crap."

Sara had to smile at his frustration. She thought him a miracle worker — it was fun to see he couldn't do everything as quickly as he wanted.

She parked in the same lot Andersen had.

"Maybe I'll check out his car while I wait for you," she said to Mason, half teasing. "Still about a half hour?"

"Funny," he growled at her. "Here's an alternative. I ran his phone through two apps. First, I used his phone's barometer that measures atmospheric pressure — that gave me his altitude. Then I checked it with an app that measures height with Wi-Fi signals. He's either on the seventh or eighth floor. I can't do any more until I break into their #%@#@@! front desk."

"I take back everything I was thinking about you, Mason. You are a genius!"

"Of course I am," he said. But Sara could hear pleasure in his voice. "Are you going in?"

"I'm thinking about it," she said. "If it were a cheaper hotel, I'm pretty sure I could smell him through the door. But maybe I can get a scent off of the door handles. It's worth a try."

"Unless someone looks out and sees you sniffing all the door handles on the floor."

"Unless that," she agreed.

"Too bad you're not a vampire instead. They have that mind control thing." Mason altered his voice to a monotone — trying to sound like a movie vampire. "There's nothing to see here. Go back in your room."

Sara grinned and got out of her car. "That would be a convenient skill to have, wouldn't it?"

"Maybe you actually *can* do it? Who knows what powers actual werewolves have? Have you tried it?"

Sara crossed the street to the hotel. She looked thoughtful. "Intriguing idea," she said.

"Now shut up. I'm going into the hotel."

# NINETEEN

It turned out that Sara *could* get a scent off of door handles. Especially from a man with sweating hands who went in only 30 minutes before her.

"It's room 714," she whispered to Mason.

"Good, because I'm finally in. They have a mesh network so I can unlock the door from here whenever you say. But most hotels also have either a chain latch or a ball/slide security latch."

Sara had found an interesting YouTube video that showed how to defeat a ball/slide kind of latch using string. Apparently, you use a string like dental floss to get under the top and bottom ball bearings — then pull it tight, and you can just flip the lever over. All from the outside.

However, to do that, you had to open the door as much as the latch would allow and put your fingers inside to do it. This did not seem like a good idea with someone paranoid in the room.

"Do you know if police chief Willis has gotten to Mike yet?" she asked Mason.

"Should have. I called Mike's phone after you left. Willis told Mike he'd be there... about 10 minutes ago."

"Can you get inside the police 911 response system?"

"Ahead of you. I got into it while you were going in. I figured we might need to know if the cops were called from the hotel."

"Good," Sara said. "Because I'm just fed up enough with this creep to do this the old fashioned way. Unlock it. I'm going in."

"Done."

Sara carefully — quietly — turned the doorknob and opened the door to the full extent of the latch. Then she stepped back three paces. She ran at the door, building up all the speed and force her 130 pounds and werewolf strength would allow. She slammed her right heel into the door right at the exposed latch. Those latches typically have three screws going into the jamb and four going into the door — so she aimed closer to the jamb side than the door.

Screws flew out, and the door kicked open. Sara let her momentum carry her into the room, her Rugar LC9 out and ready.

The room was expensive and huge — a corner room with windows on two sides. A sofa and a queen bed were about a mile from the door, all done in soothing grays and light beiges. But the stink of fear in the room counteracted the soothing colors. There was a bar and a lounging chaise closer to the door, where Greg Andersen had apparently dumped his bag when he first came in.

He was there now, frantically pawing the inside of the bag, his hand probably grasping for a gun.

Sara closed quickly and kicked his arm that was inside the bag. Hard. The gun he'd just grabbed flew out across the room, and Andersen stumbled back. Sara moved in close and squeezed her left hand around his neck. She kept her momentum, frog-marching him backward by the neck and up against a wall. Her right hand shoved the muzzle of her pistol against his forehead — right between his eyes. Her body was hard up against him, pinning his right arm and too close for his punch or kick to carry any power.

Sara felt his body tense for action. "The trigger is already half pulled," she whispered in his ear. "You don't want to jolt me in any way with some stupid punch that would only piss me off."

His smells turned. Previously he'd been reeking fear, but now a wave of anger was added to the aroma. His teeth were clamped closed, and he hissed.

"You! What do you want?"

Sara smiled. Big. He was really pissed that he was in her power.

"Yes it's me. And I'm making a citizen's arrest."

She jerked him by the neck, pulling him forward and to the left and throwing him face down on the fancy chaise. She buried his face in a fat zebra-striped pillow and stuck her right knee — hard — into his back.

Sara realized she was enjoying this. He'd moved from slimy asshole in her mind to a man who was responsible for those two women locked in that room. And... probably... a man who'd killed Velena Davis. Or had her killed.

She also realized she'd thrown him down on the chaise so she couldn't choke him to death — the way she'd been tempted.

*Nothing's proven*, Sara reminded herself. *Not yet, anyway.*

She took a zip tie from her pocket. She grabbed both his wrists and jerked them hard behind him — harder than she needed to. She fastened the tie around his wrists and pulled it tight.

*Does it make me a bad person to be enjoying this so much?* she wondered.

And then she froze. Dead still. Because there was another scent in the room. Another man. At the open door.

# TWENTY

"Police!" she heard. "Drop the gun."

Sara took her finger from the trigger and let the gun slip until she was holding the butt by her thumb and middle finger.

"I'm going to throw it over by the bed," she said, back still turned to the door. "I can't leave it by this guy."

"Ok," she heard. "But careful. No sudden moves."

Keeping her other fingers as spread out away from the gun as she could, she slowly moved it back a little and then tossed it away from both men, about 15 feet onto the bed.

Slowly she turned her head back towards the door. The man was chunky, with a round face and Clark Kent glasses. He looked like he'd just got out of bed and threw on dirty jeans, a tee and a jacket. He was holding the standard Tulsa PD Glock 22 in his right hand — pointed directly at her heart. Sara knew those guns carried .40 caliber ammo which could easily stop a bear in its tracks. A wolf would be even easier.

"I'm making a citizen's arrest," she said to the cop. "This man fled the scene of a crime."

Andersen rolled over and sat up, his arms still tightly bound behind him. He looked remarkably calm.

"This woman broke down my door and threatened me with a gun. I demand you arrest her."

The cop glanced at the door. "You did this," he asked her.

"Yes," Sara agreed. "Who are you, and how do I know you're really a cop?"

He opened the flap of his jacket to show his badge, clipped to his waist.

"I'm detective Thatcher," he said. "You're both coming downtown with me so we can sort this out."

Sara looked at him, a little confused. He looked a little different from the picture she'd seen of him. His face was rounder. And he hadn't been wearing glasses.

"I'm glad to come down," Andersen said. "I'm looking forward to filing charges against this... woman." He said 'woman' as though it were in question. "I'm an established member of this community."

He stood and held his hands out from behind his back. "Detective, it would be a miscarriage of justice to force me to appear in public with my hands tied like this. As if I were a common criminal. I'm eager to go with you and file charges."

Detective Thatcher considered. "If you try to run, I'll have to shoot you. You understand this?"

"Yes," said Andersen.

Sara watched, unbelieving, as the detective cut the zip ties. She was about to tell Thatcher that he could ask the Police Chief about how to treat Andersen. Chief Willis should be with Mike at Andersen's house by now. But something stopped her.

Thatcher was looking directly at her. "I'll come," she said. "Willingly."

Thatcher patted both of them down, pocketing both of Sara's pistols and a knife from Andersen. Then Andersen gathered his belongings, and Thatcher walked them both out the door, his gun on them.

The three of them were alone in the elevator going down. Sara inhaled deeply, because she was confused. The fear smell from Andersen, that had coated the door handle and his room when she first entered, was almost gone from him now.

Was Thatcher working with Andersen? But she and Mason — and Mike and Nia! — all thought it had to be the captain Velena had reported to — Protich. So why would Andersen feel relieved Thatcher was here? Was Thatcher in on it too — or was he a dupe?

The three of them walked out through the lobby, as though they were friends. Thatcher's gun was no longer showing. Thatcher didn't stop at the lobby to advise them about the broken door. He just took them both on a straight walk from the elevator to Thatcher's unmarked navy Police Interceptor car, which was parked in an odd corner of the parking lot. Nobody else was parked nearby.

Thatcher opened the back door and motioned Andersen in, then Sara. He didn't seem to worry that she would attack Andersen again. Why was that?

Thatcher got in the driver's seat and moved it back all the way, taking up all of Sara's legroom. Then he turned in his seat and motioned to Andersen. "Come here."

Andersen scooted forward and moved his head to Thatcher like they were going to whisper to each other. Thatcher turned even more and rose up on his seat. He put his left hand behind Andersen's neck and pulled him so Thatcher's mouth was at Anderson's ear.

There was a blur of motion from Thatcher's right hand. It went over the seat and down. There was a glint of metal, then a gush of blood. Thatcher had a knife in his hand — and he had sliced Andersen's groin artery. Then he shoved Andersen back on his seat.

Andersen's hands fluttered, trying desperately to stop the blood — but his heart kept pumping, and the blood kept pouring.

"You snake," he said to Thatcher. "I'll get you. I have pictures..."

"Yeah," Thatcher agreed. "But I know where they are."

Sara was frozen. It made no sense. Cops didn't use knives. How would this look?

Then — suddenly — she knew. The knife was something a woman might have hidden. Only to use in the back seat with a man.

Her realization was quickly followed by two even worse problems.

# TWENTY-ONE

The first problem was Thatcher's left hand came up over the seat back with his Glock 22 and he shot Sara in the guts.

Red hot blazing pain! Much, much worse than getting shot in the shoulder. Or a leg. Tears poured out of her eyes and down her face. She gasped — again and again — in agony.

She told herself over and over she could survive this. She tried to make herself believe it.

The pain told her she was going to die. That if it didn't happen fast, she would *want* to die — to make the pain stop.

The second problem — which happened while she was hunched over her stomach, panting in agony — was a voice in her ear. It was Mason's voice — whispering but urgent.

"Sara? You're not with Thatcher. I have him confirmed elsewhere."

Sara was stunned. Her hands grasped her stomach. She was bleeding, but not gushing like Andersen. She looked over at Andersen. He was no longer gushing. He had to be dead.

Her most important task right now was to hold onto her human form. Even though her body was desperate to transform. *Not now, not now, not now,* she told herself. *Wait.* For what, she wasn't sure.

Not-Thatcher had exited the front seat and opened the door next to her. He grabbed her right hand and wiped it against a still-not-bloody part of her jeans. A part that would become bloody soon.

Not-Thatcher put the knife he'd used on Andersen in her right hand and squeezed her fingers around it. Then he forced those fingers open and let it drop. Then he picked up the knife and threw it out into the parking lot.

She was gasping and crying and desperate — because holding back the transformation was becoming the hardest thing she'd ever done.

"Don't worry," he told her. "You won't last much longer."

Then he backed out of the car, leaving the door open. He pulled out his phone and dialed as he walked away from the car.

"This is Captain Protich," Sara heard him say. "Put me in touch with Chief Willis. It's an emergency."

He walked to the front of the car and rested his back against it.

*Protich,* Sara thought. *Yes... the rounder face.*

*Now, now, now!* Sara told herself. It was crazy to feel great relief at the start of her transformation. Sara hated the pain of transforming so much she couldn't understand why she ever put herself through it. Sure, it only took a minute. But that was sixty seconds of back breaking — literal here — hell.

Now she welcomed it. It wasn't really any worse than the pain from that gut shot. And the great thing — the absolutely freaking amazing thing — was at the end of it, she would be pain free.

Transformation complete, Sara quickly and silently exited the open car door and moved around the back of the car. Wolf foot pads were silent as a grave.

She was one with the night.

Sara moved out wide, so she'd be coming back at the car a full 180 from where she'd been and from about 25-30 feet away. She should look like she was coming from an alley 100 feet away.

She started wagging her tail, mentally apologizing to wolves everywhere. She trotted slowly towards Protich — the man who had sent Velena Davis out to that trap so she would die.

Sara kept her head down. Wolf eyes glowed in the dark and she knew only a few dog breeds had the golden color of wolf eyes. She didn't want to alert him and get shot again.

*Please, god, once was enough for tonight!*

She trotted tall like a golden retriever, tail up high and wagging. Protich looked up and saw her. Then he looked back down and continued talking into the phone.

He wasn't watching as she trotted right up to him and rubbed her head against his leg. She was about three feet tall to go with her 130 pounds. Big for a wolf, but a few are bigger. Rarely, even some dogs were bigger.

Absently, Protich's hand came down and patted her head.

"Good boy," he said to her.

He was already leaning back against the car, so Sara went up on her hind feet, her paws pushing him back.

"Hey," he said, smelling mildly annoyed and mildly pleased.

He would probably get away with all this, Sara knew. Assuming he did know where Andersen kept any proof of his involvement, he could make it disappear. Maybe, *maybe* there would be enough to force him out of the force. Maybe.

Maybe it would all be put on Andersen. It was his setup, after all. But how long would he have lasted without Protich's protection?

Most important to Sara — Protich sent Velena out on a call to die. Maybe Andersen asked him to do it. Maybe not. But Protich did it.

He wasn't getting money for this — Mason was sure of it. So what was his payoff? He stole Velena Davis' life so he could keep fucking drugged, helpless women — who would do anything he wanted.

Sara wished she'd had time to get to know Velena better. Maybe share a P.I. case or two with her. She liked her.

Sara growled. Deep in her throat, deep down in her lungs, a

rumbling growl that grew louder and louder. Loud enough to be heard over the phone.

"Hey!" Protich yelled, pushing at her to push her away.

Instead, Sara opened her jaws. She let Protich get a good look at all 42 of her huge, white teeth.

She wanted, badly, to terrorize him. To make him pay for Velena. But to her surprise, she was getting no pleasure out of it. He just disgusted her. She wanted him gone.

So she leaned forward, shoved her teeth around his neck, and bit down hard. She felt the crunch of his spine. She ripped out a piece of that chubby neck flesh of his.

Sara knew she needed to transform back quickly — which meant she had to eat meat. The only meat currently available was that disgusting piece of neck flesh still in her mouth. She scrunched her wolf face as tight as she could and begged herself not to throw up. Then she forced herself to swallow. She tried to tell herself it tasted like chicken.

*Yuck! Yuck! Yuck!*

Protich fell back on the car hood. Then his body slid down to the concrete. Somehow he remained in a sitting position, but his head didn't. Attached by only the skin on the left side of his neck, it tipped over and hung upside down in front of his left shoulder.

Sara looked at him for a moment. It was a striking image — she wouldn't be surprised if some cop didn't sneak a picture of it. Pass it around the department. The idea that this image would be how the guy was remembered, finally — finally! — felt like a little bit of justice for Velena.

With that thought, Sara fell to the pavement and tried to scream from the pain of transforming back to human.

But you can't scream when you transform.

No matter how badly you want to.

When she was human again, Sara patted Protich's pockets and retrieved her two guns then ran to the back of the car. The remains of her clothes were lying there, covered in blood — hers and Greg Andersen's.

She was naked.

Cops were coming.

Sara managed to pull the shreds of her slimy, cold, sodden clothes on — plastering them down on her body with the partially congealed blood so they almost looked like they weren't in pieces.

Her nose wrinkled. She felt nausea at just the idea of dressing in Andersen's blood. Not to mention her own. It was so disgusting, she forgot about the camera attached to her jacket. Then her slimy jacket pocket suddenly started buzzing. Mason. Her hand went to her right ear, but of course, the earbud was gone in her transformation.

She pulled her phone out from the jacket pocket and answered with, "I'm here."

"Yeah, I could see that."

Sara was too tired for joking. "Not the first time you've seen me naked," she said. "Status?" She shook her head to clear it. "Security cameras?"

"No cameras where you are. Which isn't easy — Protich had to know exactly where to park. Cameras everywhere else. One caught your wolf strolling around the parking lot."

"Leave that one. It'll give them an answer for how Protich died. But I need to get to my truck now and get away."

"I broke into that system when you went into the hotel. Tell me when to shut it down."

"Now. And leave it 'broken' so they don't know what time my truck left the lot.

"Done."

Sara jumped up in the back of her truck and used the combination lock to open her cross bed tool box. She pulled out one of the packages of 8x12 painter plastic tarps she had bought and stored "just in case." Thank goodness! She opened it and spread the plastic all over the driver seat — so she wouldn't have a thick coating of blood on the upholstery.

Then she got the heck out of downtown Tulsa. Mason reported he'd fried the earbud she'd been using — in case it was found. And he dumped email addresses Mike and Nia knew. He left the one phone number they had for her.

Once home, Sara burned the clothes in her fireplace and cleaned the blood from herself and the back of her truck.

She used an oxy cleaner so CSI wouldn't be able to find any blood traces — their equipment wouldn't recognize it.

She made sure her "go" bag for her and Skidi was in her other vehicle — a Ford 350 cargo van. And that all her home alarms were set.

Then she passed out for seven hours.

# TWENTY-TWO

Two stories hit the news the next morning. One was the "shootout at 10 Victory Street," where police shot and killed three men who imprisoned and drugged young women.

The other was the death of Tulsa detective Captain Foster Protich — from a horrific dog attack. While security cameras had not been able to capture the attack, local stations were given grainy footage of a huge dog roaming the parking lot right before the attack. Residents were urged to avoid any large stray dogs.

*Just great*, thought Sara as she watched the video. *I'm a video star.*

The next morning's news brought details about street women being enticed with offers of staring in advertising videos — then drugged, imprisoned and coerced into porn. Investigators found 23 women on videos they captured at 10 Victory Street. Detectives were now attempting — thus far unsuccessfully — to identify each of them. Canine units were checking the backyard for graves as only two women were found alive in the house.

By afternoon, national TV watched as women's bodies were removed from the backyard. Twenty-one of them. More news followed each day as another woman was identified from the bodies.

They were runaways and women living on the street. Women who would listen to money offered for a role in a "movie." Women who found the door in was then locked both literally and through drugs. Women who lived only as long as they were entertaining enough on film.

Keeping the story alive on national TV were revelations about the tunnel that connected 10 Victory to the house of murdered Greg Andersen.

The shocker to Sara was the police find of $2.6 million spread over three Caribbean accounts controlled by Greg Andersen.

"How did you miss those accounts?" Sara asked Mason.

"He was supernaturally smart," Mason answered in as irritated a voice as Sara had ever heard from him. "He set up the accounts in person under a different name over 10 years ago, and they just sat there, waiting for him. Four years ago the money started pouring into them. But he never went there again or called there. He only checked his balance once a year that they've found — and only from a library computer in Texas.

"The only way it was uncovered was through a driver's license in that name — hidden in Andersen's safe deposit box. What the hell kind of a man sets up a hidden bank account under an alias six years before he needs it?"

Sara thought about it. "A man whose mom just died and left him an isolated house. He knew what he wanted right then. It just took him some time to make it happen."

"He didn't care about the money," Mason said. "He didn't spend any of it. If he had, I would have found it. It was just his escape money in case he was discovered."

Sara shook her head. "I just don't understand men like him and Protich. Or maybe I don't want to. I mean... I can understand money greed. I can even understand someone killing other bad guys to steal their money. It's wrong, but it's like two cockroaches killing each other — who really cares? But to be obsessed with abusing and harming humans? For fun?"

There was a long silence on the phone. Then Mason said, "I see Mike Walsh mentioned in the papers. He's left you completely out of it?"

"As far as the police seem to know, I wasn't there. But I know I'll be hearing from him. The last thing I told him was I was going after Andersen. He won't let that go."

"I guess that rules out you dating him?"

Sara laughed. "I'll be lucky if he doesn't assign investigators to watch me."

# TWENTY-THREE

One month after that night came the call Sara had been expecting. Mike and Nia wanted to meet with her at Lupiti Lake. The two of them came in one car. Again, the three of them got out of their cars, turned their backs to the lake, and huddled — just like they had over a month before.

Sara could immediately see a change in how Nia and Mike looked at each other. How they managed to touch each other. They were either a couple, or about to become one.

Sara felt regret at a missed opportunity with Mike. But... she admitted to herself she also felt relieved. That did not mean she had a problem with relationships. Mason might think that, but it didn't mean it was true. Did it?

Sara smiled at the two of them. They would be great together.

"First," Nia said, tears welling in her eyes, "I need to say — I *want* to say — thank you. First for mama. And then for those 23 women. And for the ones that would have come after."

Mike nodded. "It would have been so easy to write it off. It seemed so small."

Compliments just made Sara uncomfortable. She shook her head and waved them off. "I'm just learning I have to trust my gut over my head."

She turned to Nia. "How are the two women doing?"

"They've got problems. Their addiction first, then what was done to them. But they've got a champion. Someone anonymous has paid one of the leading female psychiatrists in town to work with both of them."

Sara nodded.

Nia's brow furrowed. "You wouldn't know anything about that, would you?"

"Anonymous sounds anonymous to me."

Sara turned to Mike. "So, when are you leaving the department?"

"Actually... I thought I'd stay a little longer. Give it a better go." He looked at Sara. "But you suspected that, didn't you?"

"You made a real difference here," she told him. "I thought you might find that worth dealing with the bureaucracy."

"So..." said Nia, drawing out the word. "You went after Andersen. What happened?" Her expression was eager. Mike's expression was more guarded.

No matter how hard Sara had tried over the past month, she hadn't been able to come up with a story that didn't have holes in it. She picked her best truth/lie combo and crossed her fingers.

She told them about busting down Andersen's door. That he had already called Protich. She told them about Protich putting them both — unshackled — in the back of his car. She told them how confident Andersen had seemed that his troubles were over as soon as Protich arrived.

She described the knife Protich used on Andersen and her shock. Being careful to show no signs of lying, she said when she saw the knife lunge, she dove out the open car window next to her and ran to her truck and got the hell out of there.

There had been no door handles in the back seat of Protich's car, so saying she went out the window was her only option. There was no way Protich would have left the back seat door open when he got into the front.

Mike looked at her skeptically. "You ran? You — who were about to drop your guns in front of the killer holding Nia?"

Sara grimaced. "I can be courageous when there are people to save — someone to help. But there was nobody in that car worth saving. Nobody worth risking my neck for."

Nia looked at Mike.

"So the back seat window was open?" he asked.

"Yes, lucky for me."

"Wonder why it was closed when officers got there?"

"I have no idea what he did after I left. Maybe he closed it so he wouldn't be criticized for leaving it open?"

Mike started to say something, but Sara raised her hand, trying to change the subject. "No, I didn't see any dog around there, either."

"But you have a dog?"

"Of course I have a dog. Everyone should have a dog. But she's not even close to the size of that thing I saw on the TV."

She put her hand on Mike's shoulder.

"Mike, let me ease your conscience. I didn't kill Protich. And I didn't have a dog — mind you a trained killer dog — just waiting in the wings while we first broke into Andersen's house and later when I broke into his hotel suite."

Mike looked at her. "I know," he said. "But that dog being there at that time was a huge coincidence."

Sara looked at him. "You know what I thought when I saw that dog on TV and heard what it did? I thought — the devil came. He wanted to claim his own."

Sara said her goodbyes to the couple and left after that.

Mike had to know there was no logical way that Sara could have had a killer dog just waiting.

But Sara knew he was too good a cop to believe in a hellhound just happening to be in downtown Tulsa at the exact moment Sara and Protich were together — and Protich was killed.

Sara determined to stay off his radar in the future. To the extent she could — given she lived and worked in the town. Which might have to change.

Sara loved Tulsa. But she already had an FBI agent here looking for her. Now she had a suspicious police detective — who knew her identity. She needed to consider other locations.

Sooner, rather than later.

But two women were safe tonight. And so were future others they would have destroyed. She'd take her victories where she could — even though she felt guilty 21 women had died before she uncovered this cesspool.

## THE END

What's next for Sara? She never planned to use her P.I. license for anything other than to back away cops. But when someone tries to kill a friend, Sara can't say no. Soon she's up to her snout in hired assassins and explosives — because money is no object to the man who wants her first client — and now Sara too — dead. Grab your copy of Werewolf for Hire, Book 1 of the Sara Flores, Werewolf P.I. series.

WolfLady.net

# AUTHOR'S NOTE FOR THE STENCH OF FEAR

Just in case you think I made up that ridiculous list of "indicators someone is lying" — passed out by the private investigator instructor — unfortunately, I'm not.

One of the really fun aspects of writing is I get to research/investigate anything that might fit into my stories.

I thought it would be smart (and fun!) for Sara to get a private investigator license, so I took two online classes for P.I.'s.

I would have taken more -- and may still — but...

The eye-rolling items in that list came directly from a real (online) classroom for real private investigators.

Really.

# SNEAK PEAK AT THE NEXT SARA FLORES, WEREWOLF P.I. NOVELLA

By Sue Denver

Lillian Knudsen shook yet another hand and gave yet another distracted smile. The Tulsa Chamber of Commerce rubber chicken lunch sat uneasily in her stomach — a burp just made her re-taste it. She patted her red hair to make sure it wasn't falling out of the biz-exec bun she always wore to events like this — so much fussier than normal.

She'd chatted up the Caskcuts, who were at her table for the lunch. They'd bought the downtown hardware store and were hoping to learn more about how business operates in Tulsa.

She'd made the rounds of hellos to everyone else.

All she really wanted to do was get to her Jeep, go home and pass out. Except... she was afraid to sleep. Afraid the dreams would come again. Like they had for the past two weeks.

Fourteen years ago, a bomb blew up the truck she was driving in Iraq and took her left foot. She'd had nightmares about it for five years — waking up in soaking wet sheets with her heart racing.

Bo Knudsen had been there for Lillian — in the hospital, then in marriage, and finally as her partner in their shooting range business. When cancer took him two years ago, she didn't know how she managed — only that the demands of the business kept her out of the hole she wanted to crawl into.

Love for Bo — and the life they built — had made the nightmares go away so long ago she'd stopped thinking about them.

Two weeks ago, they came back. Which is why she was craving sleep at 1:30 in the afternoon.

A hand grabbed her shoulder. Lillian flinched.

"My goodness," said Betty Sue Franken, her helmet hair gorgeously styled as always and probably hard as a rock. "I didn't mean to scare you."

Lillian winced.

"I just wanted to say it's always good to see you. We women business owners have to stick together, you know." Betty Sue actually winked at her, then patted her on the shoulder. She turned to greet someone else before Lillian could even respond. Just as well.

Lillian spotted Warren Caddel, owner of Sharp Shooters gun shop, across the room. She turned away. The annoying man was trying to buy up half of Tulsa.

She shouldn't have come today. She usually liked these events. It was fun playing business leader in town — not a role she'd ever imagined for herself. She'd always thought she'd be a nurse — until Desert Storm hospitals changed her mind.

Lillian had adjusted her left leg prosthesis today to allow her to wear low heels with her best business suit. But she'd been in a rush and, apparently, she hadn't adjusted it perfectly — her left leg was tilted for a slightly higher heel than the one her shoe had.

It was frustrating how the tiniest difference could make walking feel unnatural.

She waved goodbye to the others, then took the garage elevator up a floor. She walked towards her bright red Jeep Wrangler hardtop, parked about 20 cars away.

She winced as she saw the two-week-old mashed-in front hood she had yet to get repaired. It looked like someone had swung a baseball bat down on it, but why? It made no sense.

A car engine revved behind her, so she moved over closer to the cars on her left to give the driver more room to get by.

Something hit her good right leg, crumpling it. Her body flew forward, slamming into a blue Chevy, bashing her head on the trunk.

She slid, dazed, to the dirty concrete floor.

*What the heck?*

*Who?*

Lillian looked around. She was on the floor, her head leaning against the back of the Chevy.

Tires squealed so she stuck her head out and looked. A red taillight turned the far corner, speeding towards the exit.

Gone.

Lillian saw blood on her knees, her nylons scraped to shreds. She stared blankly at them.

Suddenly, her stomach dropped. She was flying through the air from bombs, hearing the staccato of rifles shooting, the M14s returning fire. There were screams. Terrible screams. The stench of smoke was everywhere. Her silk blouse was wringing wet, and her heart was having hysterics.

She covered her head and ears with her hands and arms and pulled her head down to her knees.

"Not there. Not there. I'm not there." She said it over and over like the V.A. therapist had suggested to her.

She didn't know how long she stayed, sitting on the dirty concrete floor, arms over her head.

The next thing she noticed was the chime of the garage elevator. Someone was getting out. She shook her head and tried to stand. Her right leg hurt, but it could hold her. Her prosthesis wasn't damaged.

Lillian brushed off her legs and skirt and walked the rest of the way to her Jeep. She flashed the Jeep remote, entered and buckled up. She sat there, taking deep breaths, trying to slow her heart rate.

A gun! She needed a gun to protect herself!

Only then did she feel the Springfield Armory 911 she had holstered at her back. Sitting there. Still holstered.

Angry at herself, she leaned forward and pulled it out. She stared at it and shook her head. What was the point of going armed if you forgot it was there when you needed it? Bo would have been disappointed in her. *She* was disappointed in her.

She laid it on the seat beside her. After more deep breaths, she checked the rearview mirror and backup camera carefully.

Lillian looked everywhere when she exited the garage, but no cars sat idling — waiting for her. She was on edge the entire drive home. Cars moving towards her caused her hands to clench — she expected them to swerve into her. She was afraid of cars coming up from behind her. She flinched when cars passed her, expecting them to jerk the wheel into her.

She almost cried in relief when she finally spotted her comforting red brick house with its wide swath of green lawn and green foundation plantings. The green always soothed her, reminded her that although the temperatures could boil past 100 here in Tulsa, she was not — absolutely not — still in that hellhole Iraqi desert.

The remote opened the garage door and welcomed her back into the womb. Sanctuary. The place Bo bought for them. One story, so she never had to deal with stairs. A pool in the back, which he was so proud of. But which she hadn't used in the two years since he died.

Lillian got out of the car and found herself staring — again — at the dent on her front hood. Her peace evaporated. Nausea started to rise in her throat.

Turning purposefully away from it, she used her gun to enter her own house as though it were enemy territory. She went through it carefully, checking all doors and windows. Checking under beds and in closets. Resetting the house alarm for the night.

Satisfied she was safe — for now — she sat down on Bo's big recliner. Paws, the black alleycat with white feet Bo had adopted, jumped up in her lap and started to purr. She petted the cat, and finally, finally, her heart rate slowed back down.

She slept like a rock that night. She wasn't sure if it was physical or mental exhaustion, but a full night of sleep did wonders. She went to work feeling positive for a change.

Maybe she'd turned the corner?

But... Lillian jumped at noises. She patted her gun behind her back obsessively. She felt like her 22-year-old self again — afraid of everything. Vulnerable.

She hadn't turned any corner.

By 4:30 that afternoon, Lillian gave up. Her problem wasn't going away. Somebody had — probably — hit her car with a baseball bat. Yesterday, someone had slammed their car into her. She needed a professional to find out what the heck was going on here. And to fix it.

## Chapter Two

Sara Flores liked BK's Shooting Range. If you needed to carry a firearm, and Sara did, then you needed to practice. She had tried other local indoor ranges but came away covered in black lead soot — which meant she was also inhaling it. She really didn't want or need anything that could make her stupider than she sometimes already was.

At BK's range, you only shoot BK's ammunition which had lead-free primer plus copper bullets. Clean air.

Sara liked their pistol booth four — which was mostly hidden from the other booths. Hidden was important because Sara's reflexes were better than human. Noticeably better.

It wasn't any fun coming in twice a week just to hit the bullseye with all 60 rounds. Her vision was normal, but her muscles held her hand unnaturally steady.

Others might be satisfied shooting this well, but Sara wasn't. She worried she needed to be better.

It was a year and a half since she was turned werewolf by a Lupiti shaman who then died on her. In that time Sara mounted seven rescue missions — each to help some innocent targeted by someone evil who thought he could use them or kill them without consequences.

She'd succeeded in each of those missions — but luck played a bigger factor than she was comfortable with. Sara still worried she wasn't good enough. She had no special forces training. No martial arts.

She'd recently earned her Private Investigator license for Oklahoma, but what did that really mean? It required only 55 hours of training and passing a test. Voila! — she was now a P.I. She felt like she'd "earned" one of those mail-order diplomas sold on the Internet.

So Sara came to BK's twice a week — trying to get better. She liked to practice drawing a pistol from her different concealed carry holsters. From the front and then the back, right hand then left. That was 40 shots. Then she used her corset holster, which fit right up under her breasts. Ten shots with the right hand, then 10 with the left. As fast as she could.

Sara hit the button to bring the target back to her.

She wasn't perfect today. For a change, she'd tried shooting from a different start. She had turned past 90 degrees from the target — as far as she could while still clearly seeing it from her peripheral vision. Most of her shots were no longer dead center, and two had just missed the bulls eye. Something to work on the next time she was here.

Sara packed up and left the booth.

She was walking past the front desk when Lillian Knudsen, the owner, called her name. Lillian was a conservative woman with long red hair tied back at her nape in the kind of ponytail women wore when they were no longer in their 20s. Not high up like a real pony's.

Word was Lillian and her husband started this range when they returned together from serving in Iraq. For the past two years, Lillian ran it herself. Sara liked her quiet confidence in dealing with the occasional gun nut who demanded to use his own ammo.

Lillian held out a folded paper towards Sara. "You left this on the desk when you paid," she said, looking intently — strangely — at Sara.

"Oh," Sara said. She walked to the counter and took the paper. It looked like one of the payment receipts given out at BK's Range. "Thanks."

Lillian immediately looked down as though she were working. Sara took the hint and walked out the door, putting the paper in her purse.

She didn't want to drive all the way home before reading it, so she pulled her Ford F-150 over at the bright red "Cane's" sign and got into the drive-through for Raising Cane's Chicken Fingers. She got her usual Three Finger Combo with unsweetened tea for an early dinner. She backed into a parking spot where she could see everyone and dug in. In between bites, she opened the paper from Lillian.

It read: "I heard you're a new P.I. Call me at this number and tell me where to meet safely away from here. Now, if possible. Urgent."

Sara's eyebrows raised. This was unexpected.

Click HERE to continue reading *Werewolf for Hire.*

**Werewolves and Holidays**

Sometimes I write poor Sara Flores into a corner and even I can't figure out how she's going to survive. That's when I take a week off and write a short story. Typically about a case involving her and some holiday.

I offer the story exclusively to anyone who joins my monthly author mailing list. (It's not available elsewhere.)

You can get your free story by going to: SueDenver.com. Right on the home page there will be a story for the current holiday and a signup to get it for free. Which holiday? You won't know until you check it out!

# ALSO BY SUE DENVER

Series: Sara Flores, Werewolf P.I.

**BOOK 1: Will her first case be her last?** Lillian
Knudsen, a war vet and amputee, has someone out to
kill her. Werewolf Sara Flores got her P.I. license for
one reason — to give cops an excuse why they might
find her near dead bodies. It turns out evildoers who
attack innocents aren't interested in giving them up
without a fight. But Sara can't say to to Lillian, and
soon she's up to her snout in hired assassins and
explosives — because money is no object to the man
who wants Lillian — and now Sara too — dead.
[Novella - 146 Pgs.]

**BOOK 2: When a billionaire wants you dead - How will you survive?** Private Investigator Sara Flores was hired to find a woman who left her Tulsa casino job 192 days ago - and hasn't been seen since. The cops say Alaska Brown left willingly. The FBI isn't looking. And now, someone deadly is trying to kill off Sara and her team. Someone with unlimited funds. Has she the right to risk all their lives? But… how can she not? Can Sara and her 3-person team of misfits really take down a billionaire — or is this the case that gets them all killed?

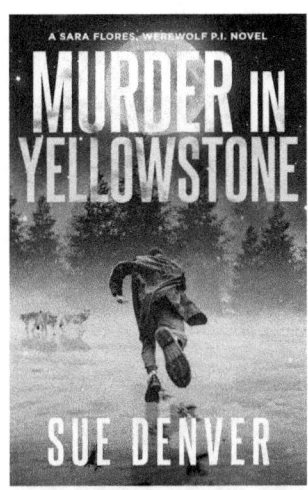

A SARA FLORES, WEREWOLF P.I. NOVEL

**MURDER IN YELLOWSTONE**

**SUE DENVER**

**BOOK 3: Murder, blackmail, and a female werewolf running loose in Yellowstone Park.** Sara Flores, werewolf P.I., needs to find a young woman who disappeared seeking evidence her father was murdered 12 years ago — instead of dying drugged and stupid in a Wyoming snowstorm. But to do that, Sara has to confront a man who even U.S. presidents have been afraid to touch. [Novel]

Series: Sara Flores, the Early Years

**BOOK 1: Abandoned. Nobody to show her the ropes. How will she use her new powers?** Nobody believes werewolves exist. Neither did Sara Flores until her Lupiti neighbor turned her. He then had the unmitigated gall to die on her, before telling her anything about what to expect. Sara determines to use her new skills for good. But besides saving innocents, what exactly does that mean? Yes, she can track down bullies and evildoers. But, is it okay to kill them? If so, is it okay to eat them? How about if she's really, really hungry? *[Collection: All 7 WolfLady short stories plus one novella — Curiosity Kills. 214 pgs.]*

BOOK 2: **Payback is a bitch!** Collection of three
werewolf vigilante novellas in one book. Rescuing
those in need isn't all Sara Flores likes about her new
life as a werewolf. Who knew it would be so much fun
terrorizing evil doers? The looks on their faces when
they discover they're not invincible — it just warms a
girl's heart. Novellas included: *Betrayal in Oklahoma*,
*Amateur Assassin*, and *The Stench of Fear*. [210
Pgs.]

# ABOUT THE AUTHOR

Did you ever want to be more than yourself? I always have. As a kid, I imagined I lived up in the clouds with a band of other kids. We would swoop down — because we could fly! — and rescue people in trouble. And we'd beat the crap out of their abusers.

When I got older, I became obsessed with crime and mysteries. I wanted to know how someone could track down evil doers and expose them to the world.

The day I quit my corporate job — my dreams came true. Today I spend my days throwing my character, Sara Flores, at one criminal mastermind after another — just to see what she can do.

And... I cheated. I let her be more than herself by making her a werewolf — the only magical creature in a world otherwise just like ours. Because I wanted to see what she could do with a wolf's senses and strength. And wildness.

So join me for stories of ruthless criminals, suspicious cops, and

Sara's small band of misfits fighting to save us all. Test drive my world with a free story at SueDenver.com.

www.ingramcontent.com/pod-product-compliance
Lightning Source LLC
Chambersburg PA
CBHW050359030726
47503CB00006B/1925